Shine With Me

Also From Kristen Proby

Bayou Magic:
Shadows
Spells

The Big Sky Series:
Charming Hannah
Kissing Jenna
Waiting for Willa
Enchanting Sebastian

Kristen Proby's Crossover Collection
Soaring With Fallon: A Big Sky Novel by Kristen Proby
Wicked Force: A Wicked Horse Vegas/Big Sky Novella by Sawyer
Bennett
All Stars Fall: A Seaside Pictures/Big Sky Novella by Rachel Van
Dyken
Hold On: A Play On/Big Sky Novella by Samantha Young
Worth Fighting For: A Warrior Fight Club/Big Sky Novella by Laura
Kaye
Crazy Imperfect Love: A Dirty Dicks/Big Sky Novella by K.L.
Grayson
Nothing Without You: A Forever Yours/Big Sky Novella by Monica
Murphy

The Fusion Series:
Listen To Me
Close To You
Blush For Me
The Beauty of Us
Savor You

The Boudreaux Series:
Easy Love
Easy Charm
Easy Melody
Easy Kisses

Easy Magic
Easy Fortune
Easy Nights

The With Me In Seattle Series:
Come Away With Me
Under the Mistletoe With Me
Fight With Me
Play With Me
Rock With Me
Safe With Me
Tied With Me
Burn With Me
Breathe With Me
Forever With Me
Stay With Me
Indulge With Me
Love With Me
Dance With Me
Dream With Me

The Love Under the Big Sky Series:
Loving Cara
Seducing Lauren
Falling For Jillian
Saving Grace

From 1001 Dark Nights:
Easy With You
Easy For Keeps
No Reservations
Tempting Brooke
Wonder With Me

The Romancing Manhattan Series:
All the Way
All It Takes
After All

Shine With Me

A With Me In Seattle Novella

By Kristen Proby

1001 DARK NIGHTS
PRESS

Shine With Me
A With Me In Seattle Novella
By Kristen Proby

1001 Dark Nights
Copyright 2020 Kristen Proby
ISBN: 978-1-951812-11-9

Foreword: Copyright 2014 M. J. Rose

Cover photo credit © Annie Ray/ Passion Pages

Published by 1001 Dark Nights Press, an imprint of Evil Eye
Concepts, Incorporated

Sign up for the 1001 Dark Nights Newsletter
and be entered to win a Tiffany Key necklace.

There's a contest every month!

Go to www.1001DarkNights.com to subscribe.

**As a bonus, all subscribers can download
FIVE FREE exclusive books!**

One Thousand and One Dark Nights

Once upon a time, in the future…

*I was a student fascinated with stories and learning.
I studied philosophy, poetry, history, the occult, and
the art and science of love and magic. I had a vast
library at my father's home and collected thousands
of volumes of fantastic tales.*

*I learned all about ancient races and bygone
times. About myths and legends and dreams of all
people through the millennium. And the more I read
the stronger my imagination grew until I discovered
that I was able to travel into the stories... to actually
become part of them.*

*I wish I could say that I listened to my teacher
and respected my gift, as I ought to have. If I had, I
would not be telling you this tale now.
But I was foolhardy and confused, showing off
with bravery.*

*One afternoon, curious about the myth of the
Arabian Nights, I traveled back to ancient Persia to
see for myself if it was true that every day Shahryar
(Persian: شهریار, "king") married a new virgin, and then
sent yesterday's wife to be beheaded. It was written
and I had read, that by the time he met Scheherazade,
the vizier's daughter, he'd killed one thousand
women.*

*Something went wrong with my efforts. I arrived
in the midst of the story and somehow exchanged
places with Scheherazade – a phenomena that had
never occurred before and that still to this day, I
cannot explain.*

*Now I am trapped in that ancient past. I have
taken on Scheherazade's life and the only way I can
protect myself and stay alive is to do what she did to
protect herself and stay alive.*

*Every night the King calls for me and listens as I spin tales.
And when the evening ends and dawn breaks, I stop at a
point that leaves him breathless and yearning for more.
And so the King spares my life for one more day, so that
he might hear the rest of my dark tale.*

*As soon as I finish a story... I begin a new
one... like the one that you, dear reader, have before
you now.*

Prologue

~Sabrina~

"We're out of tampons," my assistant, Melanie, says with a sigh. "Again."

"There's some in the office," I reply as I open paper bags and line them up on the table. "Someone delivered a whole pallet of them this morning."

"Thank God." She hurries away to fetch the feminine hygiene products.

We've been filling bags full of tampons, pads, wipes, and encouraging notes all morning. We do this once a month and then deliver the goods to the area middle and high schools. Tomorrow, we'll pack the same sacks full of healthy snacks and then make another delivery, this time including the elementary school.

Helping kids has become not just a passion for me over the past ten years but also an obsession.

I turn to start gathering more panty liners from a box when I see him walk into my storeroom. Tall. Broad. Disheveled blond hair. And more handsome than any one man has the right to be. A blast from my sordid, better-left-forgotten past. And yet, a sight for sore eyes.

"Are you lost?" I ask and watch a smile slide over his devastating face. How it's even legal for a man to look like that, I have no idea.

"I found what I was looking for," he says and pushes a hand into his pocket. His other hand, a gold wedding band glinting on his finger, holds a large envelope. "How are you, Sabrina?"

"I'm great, and curious as to what brings Luke Williams into my storeroom in Bend, Oregon."

"I came to see you," he answers. "You're more beautiful than ever, my friend."

I narrow my eyes at him. When we starred in a series of films together years ago, Luke and I got close. Since then, we've left the spotlight—him to work behind the camera as one of the most sought-after producers in LA., and I left Hollywood altogether.

And never looked back.

"As lovely as it is to see you, I don't think you're here just to catch up. Why are you here, Luke?"

He extends the envelope to me. "I have something I want you to read."

I pull out a movie script. Without even reading the title, I pass it back.

"No, thanks."

"I know I haven't seen you in years."

"Fifteen of them, give or take," I agree, nod, and go back to filling paper bags. "If you're going to try to talk me into something, you can at least help me here. These bags won't fill themselves."

"Happy to."

Melanie returns with two big boxes of tampons and almost drops them when she sees Luke.

"Thanks, Mel. Can you give us a minute, please?"

"Is Luke Williams standing here, or am I having a throwback hallucination from my college days?"

I laugh as she sets the boxes on the table. "He's here. You're not hallucinating."

"Okay. Have a good talk." She smiles and waves awkwardly, tucks her hair behind her ear, and practically stumbles over her feet as she turns to walk away.

I roll my eyes.

Luke grins.

"You can put five tampons in each bag," I instruct him. "Unless touching *girl* things weirds you out."

"I live with a house full of women," he replies, as smooth as silk, and starts divvying up the tampons. "Shawn O'Callaghan and Nora Perry co-wrote the script based on Nora's bestselling book. The lead female character was made for you, Rina. When I read the book, I immediately thought so, but then I read this script, and no one else will do for it. It has you written all over it."

"Luke, I don't act anymore. I haven't in a long time."

"You're one of the most talented people I know," he interrupts, and I don't know what to say. That's high praise coming from Luke Williams. "The way things played out was bullshit, and you got hosed."

I got more than that, but there's no reason to go into that right now.

"I have a life here, out of the spotlight. And I like it very much."

"I respect that," he says with a nod and continues filling bags as if he does it every damn day. "Trust me, no one gets it more than me. But this role, this film, needs you. Just read the script. If you decide it's horrible and you wouldn't touch it with a ten-foot pole, I'll look elsewhere."

I narrow my eyes at him. "Why now?"

"It's time."

I never could tell this man no. We never had a physical relationship, despite what the tabloids said. But our friendship was strong, and I trusted him deeply.

Still do.

"I'm just asking you to read it before you shove it back in my face."

"I didn't *shove* it." I sigh. "Okay. I'll read it and let you know. Is it a horror?"

"Thriller," he says. "And you'd play the lead FBI agent, hunting a killer. She's badass."

"I'm not in shape for that kind of role, Luke. I used to be, back when we were hunting vampires, but it's been a long time, and I haven't worked out—"

"We'll take care of that," he interrupts. "Just read it. If you're in, come to Seattle, and I'll take care of the rest."

"Why do you have to be so charming?"

He flashes that smile that could light up all of Texas during a power outage.

"I'll be expecting your call. Now, what do we do next?"

"You don't have to stay and help."

"If I do, I can ask how you are and catch up with you. I've missed you, Rina."

Damn it. "I missed you, too."

* * * *

It's good. It's really good.

I set the finished script on the coffee table and pad into my kitchen for another glass of tea.

I should text him and tell him that I've read it, and my answer's still no.

But he isn't wrong. I could picture myself in the role from the first page. The heroine's tough and fearless. Completely badass. And has a vulnerable side, too.

I want to play this part so badly, my chest hurts.

Mel can take care of the kids' program. She knows as much or more than I do. I have no family here. No pets.

I could be gone for the six months it'd take to get into shape and film.

"Damn you, Luke Williams."

I was never going to do this again. I'm opening myself up to scrutiny and gossip. But acting is in my soul, and I've missed it so much.

I reach for my phone and dial Luke's number.

"Hi, Sabrina," he says. "What did you think?"

"You know I want this role, damn it."

He chuckles in my ear. "I'm glad to hear it."

Chapter One

~Ben~

"I'm not taking any new one-on-one clients," I say to Luke as I shuffle papers on my desk. "I have a full schedule and a business to run. I don't have any extra hours in the week."

"I'll pay you one hundred thousand dollars to clear that schedule and work exclusively with Sabrina," he interjects, and my jaw drops. He can't be serious. I stare out the glass door to the gym beyond as a couple of guys spar in the ring.

"You're kidding me."

"I'm not. I need her in shape for a role within six weeks. Meal plan, exercise regimen, the whole thing. And I want you."

"Why?"

"Because you're close to the family, and I trust you not to spill a bunch of bullshit to the tabloids. Also, because you're good at your job. Rich McKenna would never have sold his gym to you if you weren't."

I sit back in my chair, still stuck on the notion of a hundred grand. As a new business owner, *of course* I could use the money. But I'm not someone who cheats my clients.

"That's too much money, Luke."

"The studio's paying it," he replies easily. "Not me. Besides, we're asking you to completely rearrange your schedule, shuffle clients to other trainers... It's an imposition. This is an investment in the talent for the studio. Do you know anything about Sabrina Harrison?"

A sexy brunette vampire hunter is hard to forget. "I mean, I know she used to be an actress. I haven't seen her in anything in a while. That's about it. I don't pay attention to that shit."

"You just proved my point."

"When would you need me to start?"

"Monday."

I sigh and rub a hand down my face. "That's in four days, Luke."

"She just took the role last night, man. You were my first call this morning. What do you say?"

A hundred grand.

"I'd better get off the phone so I can shuffle things around and be ready by Monday. But just to warn you, I'll need at least half a day each week to handle office work at my desk. This place doesn't run itself."

"Understood. You'll have time for that. I'll have you meet Sabrina at our place on Alki Beach. She'll be staying in Natalie's old house while she's in Seattle."

"What am I working with here? How much weight does she have to lose?"

"Not much. I'd say it's mostly sculpting and strength training. She needs to be ready for the role of a kick-ass FBI agent hunting a killer."

That actually tells me a lot. I make some notes, ideas already taking shape in my head.

"Text me the address, and I'll be there at eight on Monday morning."

"Excellent. I'll have the money wired to you today."

"You can pay me after the job is done," I reply. "I haven't done anything yet."

"Half now, and half later," he says. "Thanks, Ben."

He hangs up, and I pull up my schedule then scowl. I have twenty clients to juggle. Some won't be pleased that they're being passed to someone else. By doing this, I run the risk of losing a few. I hope they understand.

Two hours and a migraine later, my schedule is cleared, my trainers are busier than ever, and I only lost two customers.

Not too bad, all in all.

I walk out of the office to the ring and watch as Nate McKenna jabs at his sparring partner. It makes me proud to know that the former owner's son still comes to work out. That I've done something right here.

After knocking the other man down, Nate comes out of the ring and pulls off his gloves. "How's it going, Ben?"

I walk with him off to the side where no one else can hear and tell him about my new client.

"Congratulations," Nate says. "That'll be challenging and something great to add to your resume."

"Why do I feel like I'm abandoning my gym?"

Nate laughs. "You're not. You're bringing in significant money to help the business, and I suspect you'll be in here working out with her most days. I think it's a great idea. Now, I'd better get to the office before my wife fires me."

I laugh and walk Nate to the door.

"She's crazy about you."

He grins as he reaches his motorcycle and swings a leg over, settling in the seat.

"I know." He winks. "Have a good day."

He waves and pulls out of the parking lot, and I turn to see my first client of the day waiting by the door.

"Hey there, handsomest man in America," Honey says with a wink. *Honey* is her given name. She's forty-eight, married to a man twenty years her senior, and has had more plastic surgery than I can shake a stick at.

She's the gym bunny cliché, in her tight workout clothes and overbleached hair. She hits on me relentlessly but has never touched me inappropriately. Which means, I haven't had a good reason to drop her—just general annoyance. But the second she tries something, she's out of here.

"Good morning, Honey," I reply and hold the door open for her. She walks ahead of me, putting more sway in her hips than necessary before glancing back to see if I'm watching her. "Before we get started, I have to talk to you. Today is going to be our last day together for a while."

She frowns and looks down, her eyes sparkling when she raises her gaze to me again. "Are you saying you can't work with me anymore because your feelings for me are too personal to continue seeing me on a professional level? Because I feel the same way, Ben. I've felt the connection for months, and I think it's absolutely the best if we stop seeing each other this way so we can pursue something more...personal."

I swallow hard, sigh, and then pinch the bridge of my nose.

You've got to be fucking kidding me.

"I don't want to hurt your feelings, Honey, but that's not the reason. I have another job coming up that requires my full attention. Besides, you're a married woman and clearly out of my league."

Her eyes narrow. "You won't make time just for me?"

"I've had to shuffle all of my clients to other trainers. I'm happy to do that for you, as well. I just hired Kara, and she's excellent. She's been training for five years, and I think she'll be a great fit for you."

"I pay for *you*."

"You pay to be trained, and you'll pay the same, no matter who the trainer is."

Honey's hands fist, and her face trembles as she clenches her jaw and curls her lip.

She might throw a punch at me. It wouldn't shock me.

"You can take this hole in the wall and shove it right up your ass. You must be gay to turn me down, you piece of shit."

"And now you can leave and not come back."

"I don't want to have anything to do with this piece of shit place."

"Out you go, Honey."

I open the door and wait for her to leave. She glares daggers at me as she walks past, then suddenly presses her ample tits against my chest and pushes her face up toward mine.

It makes me sick to my stomach.

"You're missing out, Ben. I'm a fantastic fuck."

"I'm sure your husband thinks so."

She snarls as she walks away toward her little Mercedes. When she's sitting inside, she screams.

A blood-curdling scream as if she's being stabbed to death.

Then, she flips me off and peels out of my parking lot.

"Well," Kara says from behind me, "I guess I won't have to work with her."

"Nope." I turn to Kara and flash a relieved smile. "None of us do, thank God. Now, let's go over your new schedule."

* * * *

Sunrise is my time to get *my* workouts in. My job is physically demanding, all day long, but it's not the same as an intense session of my own—which is important to continue fitting into my schedule. I have to maintain a certain *look* for my career, and I feel better when I'm in top physical condition.

Running along the waterfront is my favorite for cardio. I could use the equipment at Sound Fitness, but I spend all day in there. Getting out into the fresh air is where it's at, rain or shine.

And in Seattle, there's more rain than shine.

Running also helps me empty my mind and think clearly.

I'm still not 100% sure that taking Luke's job offer was the right thing to do, but the gym can use the income, and my employees have promised that they can handle things while I'm mostly gone.

I plan to have the client at Sound Fitness for at least two hours each day anyway. I'll be able to check in and take care of anything that needs to be handled during that time.

I have a chef on standby, ready to start cooking the meals I request for Miss Harrison. I need to sit down with her first thing on Monday to talk about her goals and current fitness level before hammering out a final menu, but that shouldn't take long.

I hope she realizes how intense the next few weeks will be. I will approve every bite she puts into her mouth. Her body will ache, and she'll sometimes whimper in pain. I only hope she's disciplined enough to endure it without throwing the weights at my head.

I run through town, headed toward my best friend's bakery. Succulent Sweets has been a mainstay for delicious and designer cupcakes in downtown for well over seven years. Nic is the reason I moved to Seattle. She and I are from the same small town in Wyoming. I'd visited her often over the years, and finally decided to move here full-time a couple of years ago.

And then Sound Fitness fell into my lap when Nate's dad decided he was ready to sell and retire.

It's as though everything was meant to be.

It's early on a Friday, which means Nic is already in her kitchen, baking up the cupcakes for today.

I knock on the back door and then walk right in, the smell of chocolate already hanging in the air.

"Just me," I call out as I take a second to lean on the door and stretch my legs. When I walk into the kitchen, Nic smiles at me and continues stirring some batter in a bowl. "Don't you own one of those massive industrial mixers by now?"

"This is my therapy," she informs me. "Just like ridiculously long runs are yours."

I cross my arms over my chest and watch her work. "What are you doing this weekend?"

"I believe there is a Montgomery family BBQ to attend on Sunday, and I'm working tomorrow because Bailey is off with the guys on vacation."

Bailey, one of Nic's very good friends, has been filling in for Nic on the weekends. She's also married to two men.

To each their own, and it's good to see the three of them so happy.

"What about you?" she asks.

"I'll be working." I tell her about Luke's offer and the new client I'll be working with in just a couple of days.

"I think that's awesome. You've always loved one-on-one work the best. I know you enjoy owning the business, but this will kind of take you back to your roots. And it's an excellent opportunity for the gym. Good for you."

"I guess I hadn't thought of it like that. I felt bad for dumping all of my regulars onto the other trainers."

"Did they complain?"

"No. It's giving them extra income, as well."

"See? It's a win-win," she replies as she fills baking tins with batter. "I have to make extra chocolate and lemon today."

"Why is that?"

"Leo Nash requested them. It's Sam's birthday, and he wants to surprise her. It's sweet."

She marks something off on a checklist.

"What else is bothering you?" she asks.

"Does something have to be wrong for me to stop in and say hi?"

"That's usually the case," she says.

"I can't put my finger on it," I reply and push my hand through my sweaty hair. "I'm just restless."

"The last time you were restless, you moved from Wyoming to Seattle."

"Yeah, well, I'm not moving. Maybe I'm just anxious to get started on this new job."

"Maybe you need to get laid."

I shrug a shoulder. "Who the fuck has time for that?"

"Everyone, if they make time. You could always visit Club Temptation one night. There are plenty of solo women in the club."

I shake my head. Nic confided in me years ago that she and Matt frequent Club Temptation and that Matt is some kind of master with ropes and bondage. I've been curious in the past, but not enough to go.

"I'm good."

"Maybe you need a vacation."

I laugh and shake my head. "I don't need you to solve anything for me, Nic. I just wanted to come by and see you. It's been a few weeks."

"You're always welcome to stop by. Want one of these strawberry champagne cupcakes?"

"Sugar will kill you."

"Me, yes. Because…diabetes. But you? No."

"All of us."

"One cannot survive on chia seeds and kale alone, Ben. Live a little."

I laugh and walk toward the back door. Just stopping by to see Nic always lifts my mood.

"I'm good with my kale. Have a good day, Nic."

"Don't be a stranger!"

Chapter Two

~Sabrina~

I hate road trips. So many of my friends *love* to get into their cars and drive to fun destinations on vacation. I'm like, *take a plane!* You get there faster, have more time to enjoy wherever you are, and it doesn't suck.

I sigh and pop a Frito into my mouth. I'm not usually a junk food person, but what else is someone supposed to eat while driving hundreds of miles? I can't exactly sit here and eat a salad.

I bring up my best friend's number and call Zane, letting the audio flow through my car's Bluetooth.

"Why are you calling me?" he asks by way of greeting.

"I'm bored." I slump in my seat. "Talk to me."

"What are you doing?"

"I'm driving up to Seattle today. It doesn't look that far on a map. Why does it take *six hours* to drive it?"

"Too bad you can't just wiggle your nose and be there," he says and swallows. Sounds like he's drinking something. "Are you excited?"

My first call after hanging up with Luke the other night was to Zane. Not only is he my best friend, but Zane and I also grew up in the business together. We started out on a sitcom playing siblings before we even hit puberty. We've been tight ever since.

And when I left LA, Zane skyrocketed in fame. He's currently the most sought-after actor in Hollywood—as famous as Christian Wolfe or any other hot name in the industry.

I'm stupidly proud of him.

"I'm nervously excited," I reply. "I haven't acted in over a decade. What if I suck at it?"

"You don't," he replies easily.

"And what if the trainer is a complete asshole?"

"Luke wouldn't hire an asshole," Zane says. "I hear you crunching on something. What are you eating?"

"Fritos."

"Probably won't be on your diet, sugar."

"I know, but I'm driving for like...*days* here, Zane. What am I supposed to eat?"

"Yeah, you're not dramatic at all."

I smirk, enjoying this easy banter with my friend. It makes the miles go by so much faster.

"What were you doing? And if you tell me you were getting laid, I'm hanging up."

"I don't have the time or the patience for a woman, and you know it. I was doing my pull-ups."

"How many can you do?"

"Twenty-five before I have to rest."

"Whoa. No wonder you look all buff in the movies."

He laughs in my ear. "It's all part of the job, as you know. They pay us a lot of money to look a certain way."

"Oh, I remember distinctly. And I won't fall back into an eating disorder to be a size two, Zane. I. Will. Not. Do. It."

Throwing up, counting calories, practically killing myself and still it not being enough is something I'll never do again.

"I'd have to smack you around if you did. There are healthy ways to tone up. You don't have to be a size two."

"Tell that to the casting directors," I mumble.

"You bypassed that route this time, Rina. You're going to be great. But you're going to eat a *lot* of avocados."

"I hate avocado. Unless it's in guacamole. Does that count?"

"Sure, but you can't have chips."

"Well, damn." We laugh together, and I pass a road sign. It feels good to be able to laugh about something that was so horrible just ten years ago. "I'm only fifty-two miles from Seattle. Thank God. I've been driving *forever.*"

"What time did you leave this morning?"

"Around seven." I sigh and look in the rearview mirror. "I probably brought way more with me than I need, but I'm going to be here for six weeks."

"No break for the holidays?"

"No, working right through. It doesn't matter, Z. It's not like I see my parents or anything over the holidays."

"You see *me*," he reminds me, his voice dry as sandpaper. "What am I, chopped liver?"

"You could come to Seattle for Christmas," I offer. "I'm staying in a whole house. I'll have plenty of space."

"I just might do that. It would be good to get out of LA for a few days."

"Yay, this makes me happy. Don't call me a week before and tell me you can't make it. Just make it."

"You're damn bossy for a woman who isn't my wife or my mother."

I grin. "And you love me."

"Yeah. I do."

"Oh, thanks for the donation a couple weeks ago, by the way. That was generous and appreciated."

"Well, it's a tax write-off."

"Right. That's the only reason you sent me six figures. It has nothing to do with you being a good guy. Or wanting to help out women and children. We wouldn't want anyone knowing that."

"I'm a dick, sweets. You know that."

"That's your *reputation*. I know better. Okay, I'm starting to hit some city traffic so I'd better pay attention. I love you, and I'll see you at Christmas."

"Love you too, babe. Call me later and tell me everything."

"As always."

I hang up and bring up the GPS with the address Luke gave me already punched in. I send off a pre-typed text, alerting Luke that I'm getting close. In less than an hour, I pull my car into a driveway.

A gorgeous brunette waves from the front porch. That's Luke's wife, Natalie. I've only seen her a few times with Luke at awards shows and in tabloids, but I'd recognize her anywhere.

Luke is fiercely private. His children have never appeared in the public eye, and he makes sure the paparazzi keep their distance.

How, I have no idea.

I open the door and step out of my car, cringing at the soreness in my muscles from sitting so long.

"Welcome," Natalie says as she approaches with a big smile. "Long drive?"

"Yeah, and I'm not a road-trip girl so I'm cranky about it." I offer her a smile. "But I'm already over it. I'm Rina."

"Nat," she replies, holding out her hand for mine. "Luke's told me all about you. I'm excited to finally meet you."

"Same here," I reply.

"He's at the office this morning for a last-minute meeting so he couldn't be here, but I'm happy to give you the keys and show you around."

"Great. This is a beautiful house."

"Thank you. My parents left it to me when they passed away. When I married Luke, I didn't want to sell. And it's a good thing I didn't because this house gets so much use in our family. People come and go and need a place to call home for a while until they either buy something of their own or go on their way back home. I'm happy we have it to offer for times like these."

"That's awesome. And handy."

"Exactly." She opens the door for me. "The code and the keys are on the counter there, along with the WiFi password."

She shows me the large home. It has plenty of open space and gorgeous views of the Pacific Ocean.

"So, we're in the Alki Beach neighborhood of Seattle," she says as she leads me upstairs. "It's a fun area, with some shops and cafes. Great restaurants. It's safe to walk down by the waterfront. And you're a short ten-minute drive from downtown."

"Awesome. And who doesn't love a view like this?" I ask as I stand at the window of the master bedroom, looking out at the water.

"I know, it's the best. Please make yourself at home here. I can help you bring your things in if you'd like."

"No, it's honestly fine. I'll go at my own pace and get settled. I really appreciate you and Luke. I feel safe here."

The other woman reaches for my hand. "You *are* safe here. There's an alarm system, and we've never had issues with paparazzi. You're on the down low."

"I have been for a long, long time." I smile. "And I'd like to keep it that way."

"Well, you won't have any problems with it here."

We chat for a few more minutes before Natalie leaves. Before she waves goodbye, she lets me know that I can call for anything I might need.

It takes me an hour to unload the car and leisurely put things in their places. When that's finished, I realize I'm hungry for *real* food, so I set off in search of a nearby market.

I might as well get some groceries.

* * * *

It's Monday morning, and I've been awake for an hour. I'm on my second cup of coffee and just bit into my bagel when the doorbell rings.

He's prompt, I'll give him that.

All I know is that my new trainer's name is Ben. That's it. This should be interesting.

I open the door and am immediately under intense male scrutiny—which I expect from a trainer.

He's going to be getting me into shape.

What I don't expect are the long silence and the gaping mouth.

"Hi, I'm Ben."

I shut the door in his face and turn away, dialing Luke's number as I walk across the room.

I hear the door open behind me, but I don't turn around. I pace and mumble, waiting for Luke to answer.

Sure, gawk at the washed-up movie star, you jerk.

"Hello?" Luke says.

"Seriously, Luke?"

Suddenly, the phone is taken out of my hand, and Ben ends the call, earning a glare from me.

"I wasn't staring because you're a movie star. I was staring because I wasn't expecting you to be quite *this* gorgeous."

I prop my hands on my hips. Seems I might be speechless now, and that doesn't happen often.

"I'm Ben," he repeats.

"Sabrina."

He looks me up and down again as my phone rings in his hand. To my surprise, he answers.

"Hey Luke, Ben here. She's fine." He passes me the phone with a smirk on his cocky lips, and I press it to my ear.

"Hi."

"Everything okay there?"

"Yeah, false alarm, I guess."

"Okay, let me know if you need anything. Have a good day."

He hangs up, and I slip my phone into my pocket, then turn and lead Ben to the kitchen. Mostly, I have to look away from him so I don't make a fool of myself. Because the man is hot with a capital *H*.

I take a bite of my bagel and watch in horror as Ben takes my plate and dumps the uneaten portion into the trash.

"Uh, that was my breakfast."

"That isn't on your list of approved foods," he replies and sets a bag I didn't even notice on my counter. "But I brought supplies for a day or two until we can go over your diet, and I can have the chef start cooking your food."

"I have a chef?"

"Of course."

"Luke doesn't mess around, does he?"

"No. And neither do I. So, let's get down to business."

I sit on the stool by the island and watch as Ben starts pulling containers of food out of the bag.

"First, we need to chat," he says as he stows some things in the fridge. "I want to make sure we're on the same page and have the same goals in mind."

"I have some rules," I begin. "And I don't bend well on them."

"Okay, tell me."

He leans on the counter, and the flex of muscles in his forearms does things to me.

Focus, Rina.

"I don't starve myself."

His eyes narrow. "You're going to have so much food to eat, you won't know what to do with yourself."

I nod, relieved.

His brow creases. "Wait. What does this stem from?"

My eyes whip up to his. "None of your business."

"It's absolutely my business, Sabrina. If you have food issues, I need to know."

"I don't. Not anymore. I was anorexic for a long time when I was in the business. I guess it doesn't matter if I tell you that. It was in every tabloid for years."

He tips his head to the side, watching me. "And how are you now?"

"I'm firmly on the path away from starvation, and I actually like myself again., I'm not going back to that dark place."

"Good. Because I have plenty of food planned for you, it's just not bagels. Actually, there won't be many carbs in your diet. There will be some because we all need some, but you'll be on a protein and veggie-heavy plan. You're not vegan or vegetarian, are you?"

"If I am?"

He sighs. "It's doable, it just gets trickier. But I can work with it."

"I'm not. I just wanted to see what your answer was."

"Okay, let's go over this list, and I'll fix you a breakfast burrito."

"I can have burritos?" I feel my face light up at the idea. I'm *obsessed* with Mexican food.

"My version of them, yes."

"Why do I think our versions are different?"

"Because they most likely are. But don't worry. You're in good hands."

I'll be the judge of that.

Chapter Three

~Sabrina~

The GPS says I've driven past Ben's gym three times, but I'll be damned if I can figure out how. Because there is no gym here. Did he give me the wrong address?

"You've reached your destination on the left."

"Bullshit," I mutter to myself. That looks like a warehouse. But suddenly, a man walks out the front door carrying a duffle bag. The kind of gear a person takes to the *gym*.

Seriously? I pull into a parking space and cut the engine, looking around. Either this is it, or I'm going to get murder-death-killed.

Because this doesn't look like a gym.

I pull my bag out of the car, walk to the entrance, and open the door, shocked to see that it is, in fact, Sound Fitness.

Ben sees me right away and walks over. Yep, he's still hot as hell. No one warned me that my personal trainer, the person I would be attached to at the hip for the next six weeks, is a hottie. Towering well over six feet tall, with blond hair and blue eyes, he's attractive. Add in the muscles for days, and the devastating smile, and he could probably drop a girl at a hundred paces.

I've been around some of the most attractive men in show business, and this guy leaves them all in the dust.

It's almost annoying.

"I'm so sorry I'm late," I begin as soon as he walks to me. "I'm *never* late, but I couldn't find this place. Why isn't there a sign out front?"

"The former owner never had one. It's taken me a while to have a logo designed and stuff, but a sign is on the way."

I take a deep breath and ignore the smell of sweat. I can see that it's a well-maintained, clean place. But the smell of perspiration is always present in places like these.

I avoid them like the plague.

"I won't be late again," I promise him.

"I believe you. Go get changed, and we'll get started."

He leads me to the door of the women's locker room, and I hustle inside, choose a temporary locker, and change into yoga shorts and a loose tank top. I pull my blond hair into a ponytail, slip on my sneakers, and lock my things in a locker.

Ben's waiting for me when I come out of the locker room.

"Thanks for the extra day to get settled," I say. "It helped a lot."

"You're welcome. Starting tomorrow, I'll meet you at your house, and we'll start a morning routine there. So today was your last day to sleep in."

"I was up at six," I inform him.

"Like I said, last day to sleep in."

I feel my eyes narrow. "I'm not a morning person. And I'm not complaining, I'm warning you."

That easy grin I'm already coming to appreciate slides over his handsome face. "I've been warned, then. Okay, I'm going to warm you up with ten minutes on the bike."

He gets me situated on a stationary bike and then walks away to talk to a customer. He's distracted today, I can tell. I'm sure that being torn from his business to work with me has taken a toll on him. Luke told me that Ben owns this gym, but that it's new for him. And now I'm taking up a huge chunk of time.

I assume the studio is paying him well but it's still an inconvenience.

I hate the stationary bike. Truth be told, I hate all of the equipment in a gym. I prefer to be outside, running, biking, or even kayaking. It's one of the reasons I moved to Bend about ten years ago. There's so much to do outdoors, even in the winter. I've become addicted to cross-country skiing.

Who knew the famous little girl from dozens of movies and TV shows back in the day would turn out to be an outdoorsy hermit?

Not me, that's for sure.

But I'm not here for fun, I'm here for a job. Which means, I can't be choosy. I'll leave the how and why up to the professional.

Ben.

Bless his sexy little heart.

Just as I've started building up a sweat, he rushes over to me and grins when he sees how far I've gone in such a short time.

"You're hustling."

"I like to ride my bike," I say. "My *real* bike."

"Really? I like to cycle, too. We'll incorporate that into your routine."

I grin and follow him to the weight area.

"Cardio is going to be important because it sounds like you're going to be put through the paces with a stunt instructor, as the fights in the movie will be choreographed. You'll need the endurance for long days of training.

"But we also need to define your upper body muscles, particularly your shoulders and arms. Your character is an FBI agent badass who chases serial killers for a living, and she's going to be in top physical condition."

"Agreed," I reply with a nod. "It's the first thing I said to Luke when he told me about the role—that I'm not in shape for it. And I'm no slouch."

"Not at all," Ben agrees. "You're in great lifestyle shape."

I tilt my head to the side. "What does that mean?"

"That you can go about a normal active lifestyle without trouble. You can hike a mountain, or run a 5k, or kayak across a lake just fine. You don't need muscle definition for that. Now, protecting yourself and others for a living requires a different level of fitness."

"And we're going to get me there so I look the part for the movie."

"Exactly. We're going to start with legs today."

"I thought you said you wanted to define my *upper* body."

"And we will, but you need a solid foundation under you to

support what we'll put your upper body through. So today, we're going to work on strengthening your legs a bit, then we'll move to arms and core tomorrow."

"Okay. Let's do it."

He's not distracted anymore. All of his attention is on *me*. I don't remember the last time I had a man's undivided attention. Especially a handsome man.

It's been a long time.

And of course it happens with a guy I'm working with, in a city nowhere near where I live.

Because that's just my luck.

I focus on the tasks at hand: squats, kettlebell swings, and lunges. My legs are rubber by the time Ben ends the session.

"Shit, I'm out of shape." I pat my face with a towel. I'm a sweaty heap, and I'm exhausted.

"I worked you hard," he concedes with a smile. "Come on, I'll stretch you out."

He tosses a mat onto the floor, and I lie on my back. He pushes my legs up and then to the side. He stretches out my back and my arms.

His movements are quick and efficient, his hands strong and confident.

I really need to work on shaking off the lust I have going on here.

"Go change, and I'll take you to lunch," he says, surprising me.

"I have lunch at home."

He pats my shoulder. "Trust me, Rina."

Hearing my nickname has never sent electricity up my spine.

Until now.

It doesn't take long for me to clean up and get dressed. When I walk out of the locker room, Ben's waiting for me. I see he's changed from gym clothes into jeans and a T-shirt. His arms are ridiculous, the muscles well-defined under the sleeves of his shirt. It's cool out, so he snags a black jacket off a hook as he leads me outside.

"We're just going down the street. Mind if we walk?"

"I'm with you," I reply, walking next to him as he sets off down the sidewalk toward the heart of the city. "Did you grow up here?"

"No, I'm a transplant from Wyoming."

I glance up at him in surprise. "Really? Why here?"

"I like it here. And my best friend moved here. I visited a couple of times and decided to make the move, as well. Did you grow up in California?"

"Yep. Born and raised. Started working at three."

"That's pretty young."

"I was a cute baby. In movies by four, and on television with a contract for a sitcom by nine."

"I take it you didn't go to regular school?"

"No." I smile and dodge a crack in the sidewalk. "We had tutors on set."

"Do you still live in LA?"

"Hell, no." I shake my head adamantly. "Never again. I live in central Oregon now."

I'm sure he has a ton of questions. Everyone does. But rather than ask, he's quiet as he leads me into a restaurant. We're seated quickly.

I don't have to pay attention to being recognized anymore. For a long time, it happened *everywhere*. But now that I've been out of the business for a dozen years or more, I'm rarely recognized.

It's awesome.

It also helps that I went back to my natural blond hair color, rather than the dark hue that was part of my image for so long.

Once we're seated and have menus, Ben turns to me. "I'm going to show you how to order healthy food off a menu."

I narrow my eyes at him. "And here I thought this was just a friendly lunch."

"It's both." He slips into the booth next to me so he can share my menu, and I feel my heart beat a little faster at the close proximity. "The first thing most people gravitate toward when eating healthily is the salads. But if you look at the caloric content, some of them are worse than getting a burger."

"I'll have a burger then."

He glances at me. "Smartass. I want you to stick with high-protein meals. You absolutely could order the burger with a lettuce bun and a salad on the side with no dressing. I usually ask for a side of lemon to squeeze on the salad as dressing."

"Mm, delicious." My voice drips with sarcasm. "Don't worry, I used to count every calorie that went into my mouth. I can do this."

"I don't want you to obsess about the calories," he says, shaking his head. "You're going to be burning a *lot* of them, and replacing them is good. But I want your food choices to be deliberate."

"Got it." I scan the menu. "I think I'll have cheesecake for dessert." His head whips up at that, and I can't help but laugh. "Got you."

"You get one cheat day a week." He slips back into the seat on the other side of the table. "Save the cheesecake for that day."

"I can cheat?"

"A little. If you're craving something, do it all on that one day. Your body can't hold onto *everything* you consume in that day. If you spread it out over the whole week, you *will* hold onto the sugar and fat."

"That makes sense. Okay, I'll save it."

I end up ordering the burger with a lettuce bun but no side. If I can't have dressing, what's the point of salad?

When we're done eating and leave the restaurant, I turn to walk back toward the gym, but Ben stops me.

"I want you to meet someone. It's just across the street."

I look over and see a cupcake shop. *Succulent Sweets.*

"I'm one hundred percent sure this isn't approved for my diet plan," I say as we cross the street.

"No, ma'am."

"If you take me in there, I'll hate you."

He smirks and opens the door for me. "No, you won't."

I glare and walk in ahead of him. The luscious smell of chocolate and cherry and all of the goodness in the world assaults my nostrils.

"Hate with a passion," I mutter as we walk through the dining room to a long, glass counter full of rows and rows of delectable cupcakes. "I'm coming straight here on cheat day. Screw cheesecake."

"You're a fan of sugar, then?" Ben asks.

"Isn't everyone?"

"Not me," he says with a shrug and then grins at the pretty brunette behind the counter. "Hey."

"This is a nice surprise." She walks around the counter to hug Ben. "What are you doing?"

"I wanted to introduce you to Sabrina. This is Nic, the best friend I mentioned earlier."

"Nice to meet you," I say, offering my hand.

"Oh, and you're the new client." Nic smiles. "It's nice to meet you, too."

"Nic is related to Luke Williams by marriage," Ben says, surprising me.

"It's a huge family," Nic adds. "I'm married to Matt Montgomery, who is sort of a brother to Luke's wife. It's a story."

"They're all a little intimidating but very nice." Ben smiles. "We just had lunch across the street, and I thought we'd pop in for a minute."

"Can I get you anything?"

I whimper, making her laugh. "I'm on a strict diet plan, but I was just informed that I get a cheat day. You can bet on the fact that I'll be here on that day. This all looks amazing."

"I would love that," Nic says. "In fact, why don't the two of you come to dinner with Matt and me? Does Friday night work?"

"Is that my cheat day?" I ask Ben.

"You can pick the day," he replies.

"Yes, Friday works," I agree. "Thank you for asking us."

"I'll bring cupcakes. What flavor is your favorite?"

"All of them. I'm literally not picky. If it has sugar, I want it."

"I'll bring an assortment then." She flashes a big smile. "It's nice to meet you, Sabrina."

"Same here."

We leave the bakery and just start down the sidewalk toward the gym when I start to laugh.

"What's so funny?" Ben asks.

"Is it wrong that I'm going to work my ass off this week so I can have two cupcakes on Friday?"

"No, that's the point," he says.

"What do you eat on cheat days?"

"Pizza. Pepperoni pizza."

"Mm. Pizza."

Chapter Four

~Ben~

"So, he tried to kill me this week," Rina says as she takes a big bite of homemade pizza. The cheese is long and stringy, and she sticks out her pink tongue to catch it.

I've discovered that she also sticks out that tongue when she's pushing a heavy weight, or when she's maintaining her balance.

I've dreamed about that tongue.

Among other things.

"I think that's his job." Nic winks.

"Well, if so, he's good at it," Rina replies. "I could barely sit on the toilet yesterday. I had to get about halfway down and then just let myself drop. I don't think I've ever been that sore."

"It means it's working," I remind her and reach for another slice. Nic knows that pizza is my cheat meal, and she makes the best pepperoni I've ever had. She even makes the dough from scratch.

She's the best friend there ever was.

"It should hurt less and less as time goes on," Matt says. He walks behind Nic and runs his hand over her short hair, then gently squeezes her neck before sitting beside her.

"Not for a while yet," I disagree, earning a glare from Rina. "This is literally your *only* job right now."

"I know." She sighs. "And I'm not a complainer. But does it have to hurt so much? At least Luke's paying me well for the role. I can help a lot of girls with that money."

I narrow my eyes on her. "What do you mean?"

"I meant to ask you what you do now that you're not acting," Nic says.

"I run a nonprofit down in Bend," Rina replies. "I gather supplies for kids. We do a monthly drop-off at every school. Feminine hygiene products for girls whose families can't afford or don't bother to supply them at home. And each week, we put together snack bags for kids at all of the schools."

"Wow," Matt says. "That's a huge undertaking, even in a smaller community."

"There are hungry and underprivileged kids in *every* community," Rina stresses. "*I* was a hungry kid, and not because my family couldn't afford to feed me. Trust me, my parents did very well, thanks to my hard work. They withheld food from me because I had to look a certain way. I knew how to count calories by the time I was eight years old, and it led to an eating disorder later in life. *No* kid should be hungry, especially in a country as wealthy as ours."

"I couldn't agree more," Nic says. "And I'm so sorry that you went through that."

"Thank you. We also do clothing drives at the beginning of the school year, and we supply backpacks full of school supplies."

"And you do it all on donation?" I ask, so intrigued that I've set my pizza aside.

"Most of it," she says. "I fronted all of the money when we started, and I've hit up a lot of very wealthy people in Hollywood for donations over the years. It was particularly gratifying when I reached out to the same directors who told me I couldn't eat for three days before a scene."

"Jesus," Matt mutters. "Does that shit still happen?"

"Every day," Rina confirms. "Not just to women, either. It's a corrupt business, for many reasons. I left because I knew if I didn't get the eating disorder under control, it would kill me. And I couldn't do that *and* act in LA." She pauses and glances around. "Please don't repeat that."

"We wouldn't say anything to anyone about what you say," Nic assures her. "In addition to Luke being in the family, we have Leo

Nash, Will Montgomery, Amelia Montgomery, Kane O'Callaghan…well, you get the idea. Also, Matt's a cop and never tells me anything good."

"I tell you plenty," he retorts. Nic rolls her eyes, and Matt narrows his. "Did you just roll your eyes at me, little one?"

"Oh, yeah."

"Looks like we'll be having some fun later," he mumbles before taking a drink of his soda.

"I miss the work," Rina continues. "I know I've only been gone a week, but I enjoy it, and I miss it."

"There are plenty of shelters that could use donations," Matt suggests. "Especially women's shelters."

"You could do the hygiene packets for them," Nic says. "Oh, and what about baby bags? A ton of women leave abusive relationships with babies in tow. You could do them by age group."

"That's a *really* good idea." Rina seems to think it over. "But I think I'd need help stuffing bags and such."

"We have an army of people who would love to help," Nic says. "I know if we did a girls' night, add in some wine and cupcakes, the Montgomery women would be happy to help put things together with you."

"Really?" Rina's face lights up at the idea. "I just got an anonymous donation the other day that would more than cover the costs. I would do it all under the nonprofit umbrella that I already own, so it would be simple. I can work on it in between torture sessions with Attila the Hun here."

She points at me, making me laugh.

"That's Ben the Hun to you."

She snorts. "Matt, do you happen to know the names of a few of the shelters I can call?"

"I'll write them down for you before you leave tonight."

"Thanks."

I had no idea that Rina was a humanitarian. It should have occurred to me to ask her what she's been doing over the past several years, but it didn't. I've been attracted to her physically since the moment she opened her door and then slammed it in my face. But knowing how passionate she is about giving back to the community makes her even more beautiful.

She's gorgeous. She has a great work ethic, and she's funny.

And she spends all of her spare time helping kids in need.

If that doesn't finish the job of making me want her, I don't know what would. And I do. I want her in my bed, against the wall, in the kitchen, and anywhere else I can get my hands on her.

Not because she's famous. I don't give a rat's ass about that.

I'm attracted to *Rina*. The woman sitting next to me, gorging on delicious pizza and laughing with my friends. The woman who hates burpees and loves sugar. The woman who wants to put baby bags together for women who can't afford to buy them for themselves.

Rina's damn hot in so many ways.

"Where did you go?" Nic asks me, pulling me out of my reverie.

"Sorry. I was just thinking about tomorrow's workouts."

"Okay, that's just mean," Rina says. "I'm enjoying my cheat meal, on my rest day, and you're busy thinking about torturing me tomorrow?"

"Yes."

I grin as she glares at me and reaches for a chocolate cupcake.

"Just for that, I'm going to eat *three* cupcakes."

"That's fine. I'll have you run an extra mile tomorrow."

She bites into the cake and moans in happiness. "Oh my God. It's worth the extra mile. What do you put in these? Crack?"

"Something like that," Nic replies and starts clearing the table.

"I'll help," Rina offers, but Nic shoos her back into her seat.

"Matt and I can clean up. I'm just moving some of these dishes into the kitchen. Enjoy your sugar binge."

"Oh, I am," Rina assures her.

"I'm going to send some home with you, too."

"I have until midnight to gorge on these," Rina says. I don't have the heart to tell her she'll make herself sick. "Yay me!"

* * * *

"Do you want to come in?" Rina asks when I pull into her driveway. "Nic sent home two more cupcakes. I can't eat all of this myself."

I won't have any of that sugar, but I'll be damned if I'll resist the invitation to spend more time with her. I follow her into the house. Rina flips lights on as we walk through the home to the kitchen.

She sets her little box of cupcakes on the kitchen counter and reaches into a cabinet for a plate.

Her blond hair is down tonight, falling in loose waves to the middle of her back. She always wears it up when we work together, so seeing it down is a treat. She's wearing a light layer of makeup, and she's dressed in a pretty red sweater and blue jeans.

I could eat her alive.

Rina sets a cupcake on a plate and licks frosting off her thumb as she passes it over to me, then picks up the other one, peels down the paper, and takes a big bite.

"This has to last me a week," she says around a mouthful of food. She's halfway into her treat when she looks up and sees that I haven't touched the one in front of me, but I'm watching her in fascination. "You're not going to eat that?"

"No."

She stuffs the rest into her mouth and shakes her head. "It's a shame it'll go to waste. I can't eat any more without putting myself in sugar shock, and it won't last for another week."

As she walks around the island to retrieve the plate, her arm brushes mine as she reaches past me. I instinctively take her hand, tug, and press her against me from knees to chest.

The pupils of her gorgeous blue eyes dilate as her gaze whips to mine before moving down to my lips, which tingle under her scrutiny.

"I've wanted to do this all damn week." My lips descend on hers, light at first, just to get a taste. But when her sweet little tongue brushes against my lower lip, I'm lost, caught up in the smell, the taste, the *feel* of her pressed against me so perfectly, it's as if she was made for me.

My fingers dive into her soft, thick hair, and I hold on as I kiss her senseless. Her hands glide from my shoulders, moving down my sides to fist in my shirt.

I want to boost her up onto the island and fuck her until neither of us remembers our names.

But we're not ready for that. Hell, I'm not sure we're ready for *this*.

But I can't keep my hands off her. And I'm done trying.

She moans long and low in her throat. I come up for air long enough to nibble my way to the corner of her mouth. I kiss the dimple in her cheek and then move down to her jawline.

"You're the only sweet thing I want to taste," I whisper against her earlobe. "Jesus, you'd tempt a saint, Rina."

She leans her forehead against my chest, and we both work to catch our breath. When she looks up at me again, she's smiling.

"Did we just fuck everything up?" I ask.

"Not for me," she says. "For the record, I've wanted you to do that all week. I'm glad I'm not the only one who feels the chemistry."

"You're not the only one," I confirm. "It's almost a visible thing between us. When I stretch you out in the gym, I have very *un*professional thoughts, and that's not like me."

She giggles and hooks a piece of her hair behind her ear. "It's not like me, either."

I lean in for one more kiss, though instead of the soft, gentle peck I intended, it turns into another inferno, leaving us both panting and glassy-eyed.

"Whoa." I swallow hard.

"Yeah." She blinks slowly. "Whoa."

I grip her shoulders and set her back from me, then drop my hands, feeling immediately cold at the loss of connection.

"I should go," I say, stepping away. "I'll see you in the morning."

"What time?"

"Six. I'll have bikes with me. We're going to ride along the waterfront."

"It'll be cold," she reminds me.

"Wear a sweater," I reply. "Layers. It would be great if you could get ugly overnight as well so I don't want to kiss the fuck out of you anymore."

"I'll see what I can come up with." She's grinning from ear-to-ear now, and she's not ugly in the least. Not at all.

Not even a little.

I need a cold shower.

Chapter Five

~Sabrina~

"There will be no more kissing."

I'm staring at myself in the mirror. I have sleepy eyes, my face is clean of makeup, and my hair is up in a bun with a headband in place to keep the flyaways off my face while we ride.

I'm giving myself a stern talking-to.

"No kissing." I point my finger at my mirror image. "Yes, he's hot, and his hands are crazy amazing, and it would probably be the best sex of your life."

I frown.

"No one said anything about *sex*. Now you're taking it too far, Rina. Keep your hands and lips to yourself and just work on getting ready for this role. *That's* the job. Doing Ben is *not* the job here."

I narrow my eyes at myself and then nod once in satisfaction.

That's been decided.

Ben suggested I wear layers, and I followed orders. I'm in workout pants and a t-shirt with a sweatshirt over that. I have a scarf to put around my neck if I need it. It's winter in Seattle, which means it could be seventy or thirty.

You never know.

But I *do* know that it's cooler by the water. Though the fresh air will feel good.

I've just finished eating a bowl of cantaloupe when the doorbell rings.

It's six on the dot. He's right on time.

"Always punctual," I murmur as I unlock and open the front door. "Good mor—"

He sweeps in, pulls me against him, and plants those lips on mine. I loop my arms around his neck and let him have his way with me.

Because I'm a red-blooded woman, and Ben is hot as hell.

Hot. As. Hell.

My stern bathroom conversation goes right down the toilet as he pushes the door closed with his foot and spins me around to pin me against it.

His hands skim down my sides, then move back up again to frame my face as he thoroughly explores my mouth.

I was still half-asleep when he arrived. I'm fully alert now.

He's breathing hard when he pulls away, and his blue eyes are on fire as he stares down at me.

"Good morning," he says.

"Hi."

"I couldn't help myself."

"Not complaining." I feel the smile slowly spreading over my face. "I gave myself a pep talk earlier, explaining that we weren't going to do that again."

"Sorry, I didn't get the memo."

I swallow hard as he backs away.

"It's okay. I don't mind. Is it hot in here?"

He laughs and points at my sweatshirt. "You're dressed for cold weather."

"Right. Yeah. Okay, so we're going on a bike ride?"

"Yes. If we don't, I'll exercise you in other ways, and I don't think we're quite there yet."

"Given that I talked myself out of kissing you again this morning, I have to agree."

"You can *always* say no. No harm, no foul. I mean, I'll be a little disappointed because I'm having a hard time keeping my hands to myself, but you're in charge here."

I nod, satisfied with that statement. "Understood. So far, I'm not saying no."

"Great. Let's go for a ride, shall we?"

I raise a brow at the double entendre, and he shakes his head. "Seriously, let's get out of here."

He leads me down the sidewalk to the back of his SUV where he has two bikes on a rack. He unlatches them and sets their tires on the ground.

"We're going to ride for about fifteen miles today."

My head whips around in surprise. "Wow."

"If you get to a point where you think you've reached your max, just say so, and we'll turn back. But remember, we have to get back here, so if we're five miles in, we have to come back five miles."

"Right." I nod and accept the helmet he holds out for me. "I'm usually good for a ten-mile ride. Let's see how fifteen goes."

"Speak up if it's too far, but this is meant to be a workout."

I nod again and slip my hands into the riding gloves he also brought for me. Ben thought of everything today.

"If you enjoy this, I'll leave the bikes and gear here in the garage, and we'll make this a regular part of your weekly routine."

"Cool."

We hop on the bikes and set off. I follow closely behind him, getting a feel for the equipment. The seat is a little narrow, so my ass will likely hurt tomorrow.

I'll order a new saddle later today.

But aside from a sore ass, the ride is beautiful. It's a cool day, but there's no sign of snow, just moisture from the ocean as we ride along the mostly empty paths and roads.

Leaving so early in the morning has its benefits.

I don't even monitor my smartwatch to see how far we've gone. My legs feel strong, probably from all of the work he put me through over the past week, and my lungs love the brisk air. Before long, we've circled back toward the house and ride into the driveway.

"That was so fun." I grin as I swing my leg over the bike and reach for the water bottle secured to the bar under the seat. "The fifteen miles flew by."

"We went twenty," he says, surprising me.

"Seriously?"

"Yes, ma'am. And you killed it, even when we took those hills through downtown."

"Those burned, I'm not gonna lie. But then we get to go *down*hill, and it makes up for it. I'll go open the garage."

I hurry through the house to press the button for the big door and help Ben stow our gear. I definitely want this to be a regular thing—weather permitting.

"Let's go in and stretch you out."

"Yeah, I'm stiffening up. Why don't you ever have to stretch?"

"I do." He leads me into the living room where we have a mat set up on the floor from earlier in the week, and we both start stretching out. When it's time for my legs, I lie on my back, and he kneels between them, pushing my knees up to my chest and then to the side.

This time, his hand slides down the inside of my thigh, and he rubs gently. "How do you feel here?"

"Tight."

"Hmm." He leans in and kisses my cheek lightly. And just like that, the whole mood shifts.

And I'm not mad about it.

Those magical hands of his start to roam, and my fingers dive into his hair as he kisses me senseless.

He's just pressed his still-clothed hardness against my core when his phone rings.

He tips his forehead against mine. "Damn it."

"You should probably answer that."

"Damn it," he says again as he backs away and digs his phone out of his pocket. "It's the gym. This is Ben."

His eyes are on mine as he listens to the voice on the other end of the call.

"I'll be there in fifteen."

He clicks off and sighs.

"Emergency?" I ask as I sit up.

"Yeah. I'm sorry. You're welcome to come with me and do your weights earlier than planned, or you can just meet me there later."

"I'll meet you," I reply. "I have some calls to make. I'm getting this new venture underway today and I have some questions I need answered."

"So quickly?" he asks.

"I'm like a pit bull. Once I dig my teeth in, I don't let go. I'm excited to get started on it. You go ahead and take care of things, and I'll meet you there in a few hours."

He nods, and we both stand, but before I can turn away, he cups my cheek and kisses my forehead.

"I'll see you soon."

He walks away, already focused on whatever's going on at the gym. When the door closes behind him, I fan my face.

Ben is damn sexy. I'm totally going to kiss him every chance I get.

And I'm not sorry.

* * * *

"This cart is full," Ben says later that evening. We're at a local wholesale store, and I'm loading up on the goods. Ben eyes the flat cart I'm toting around. "And that's half-full."

"It'll be fine," I assure him. "I need more diapers, wipes, and formula."

I'm glad I took him up on his offer to join me tonight. This is a lot of stuff to lug around, and Ben has muscles for days.

When we're as loaded down as we can be, we check out. Several thousand dollars later, we make our way out to his SUV.

"This won't fit," he points out.

"Didn't you ever play Tetris when you were a kid?" I ask as I point to the big stuff first. "This will totally fit. It'll just take some effort."

Thirty minutes later, with a *very* full vehicle, we pull into my driveway.

"Now we have to haul all of this inside." I frown. "That's always the worst part. Shopping is the fun part."

"Go in," he says as we climb out of the SUV. "I'll bring it in. You just tell me where you want it all."

"You don't have to—"

Before I can finish, four other vehicles pull up behind us, and on the street, and we watch as Nic and Matt get out of one, while Luke and Nat and two other couples get out of the others.

"If I'm hosting a party, I'm *very* poorly prepared," I say as Nic approaches us.

"No, we're here to drop stuff off." Nic grins and points to the others. "I told the girls about your plan, and we all want to help. This is Jules and Nate McKenna. Jules is Matt's sister. And this is Matt's brother Caleb, and his wife, Brynna. You know Nat and Luke."

"Hi, everyone," I say, wave, and then eye their cars. "They're all full."

"Yep," Jules agrees. "We could have brought more, but we Tetrised this as much as we could."

"See?" I turn to Ben. "Tetris."

"Why don't you ladies go in and decide where you want this stuff," Nate suggests. "We'll bring everything inside."

"Sounds good to me," Brynna says. "Lead the way, Rina."

I'm dumbfounded, and I'm pretty much *never* speechless. I've never known people to just jump in and help a stranger like this.

"Where should we put the stuff?" Jules asks, looking around.

"Are you okay, Rina?" Natalie asks.

"You did *not* have to do this." I shake my head, completely overwhelmed. "I didn't expect you to spend your money and buy a bunch of stuff for charity."

"Women, babies and kids," Jules says. "That's all you had to say. Plus, it's a tax write-off. Now, where would you like it all?"

I blow out a breath and look around, formulating a plan in my head. "Okay, let's do baby stuff in the dining room. Feminine hygiene in the upstairs guest room. Snacks and other miscellaneous things in the living room."

"Got it," Luke says as he walks through carrying four boxes of diapers. He stacks them neatly in the dining room and then walks back outside for another load. Occasionally one of the guys passes something off to us to take and organize.

Within thirty minutes, all five SUVs are unloaded, and all of the items are in the house.

I watch as Nate carries a baby bassinet into the dining room, and I lean over to Nic. "Is it just me, or is that dude incredibly sexy carrying that?"

"Nate's incredibly hot doing anything." She smirks.

The man in question must have heard us because he glances our way and offers us a wink.

Well, okay, then.

"You all went above and beyond," I say as we finish up. "I mean, you even bought furniture. Bassinets, bouncy seat thingies, *four* brand new breast pumps."

I shake my head in wonder.

"We can do more." Natalie pulls me in for a hug. "I think it's awesome that you get to do this every day. We'll get some of the girls together and come over soon to organize and get it ready to deliver. And we can help with that, too."

"Don't make me cry," I plead as I pull back and glance around at the nine people standing with me. "Your family is wonderful."

"It's just what the Montgomerys do," Luke says. "They help, and they will suck you in as one of their own. You've been warned."

I laugh. "I would offer you all something to eat, or a drink, but I don't have anything here to give you."

"We have to go." Jules waves me off. "We all have kids at home who have probably burned our houses down by now. Have a good night. We'll see you soon."

"Thank you." I follow as they make their way toward the door. "Sincerely, thank you."

Caleb, the one who's been the quietest since they all arrived, turns back to me. "Thank *you*. I have daughters. It makes me happy to know women like you are looking out for them."

He nods and follows the others, and I have to close the door before I dissolve into a puddle of tears.

Ben's hands are on my shoulders, so I turn and wrap my arms around his waist, needing a hug.

"Well, that completely overwhelmed me," I say with a sniffle.

"Yeah. They do that."

Chapter Six

~Rina~

He looks tired.

It's been two days since the Montgomerys delivered all of the goodies to my place and the emergency at the gym that called Ben away. It seems a trainer walked out, quitting on the spot. Because Ben's been working exclusively with me, there wasn't any wiggle room in any of his other trainers' schedules to absorb the workload.

Because of that, he's been juggling me *and* the extra clients while simultaneously searching for a new trainer. He's been working long days, and I only see him for our sessions.

There have been no more hot kisses.

Well, there was *one* hot kiss yesterday after our bike ride. But aside from that, he's been too busy to lock lips.

Or do anything else.

Now that our afternoon session has been wrapped up, and I see him working with a guy at the bench press, I can't help but feel bad for him. His eyes look strained—the long hours are clearly catching up with him.

I walk over to the front desk where his administrative assistant sits and smile at her.

"Hey, Lisa."

"Hi, Rina. What can I do for you?"

"How late is Ben scheduled to be here today?"

She clicks her mouse a few times, looking at the computer screen. "Looks like his last client is at eight."

"He started with me at six this morning."

Lisa nods and cringes. "Yeah, the poor guy's been working nonstop. But he interviewed a guy this morning who looks promising."

"Can you give me Ben's address?"

She narrows her eyes on me dubiously. "Pretty sure I'm not supposed to do that."

"I want to take him some dinner later. I want to do something for him. *I'm* the reason he's in this mess. I promise, there's nothing sinister going on here."

Lisa thinks it over and then nods. "He could use some TLC. If he fires me, you have to have my back here."

"He won't fire you," I assure her as she writes his address on a sticky note. "Thanks, Lisa."

"You're welcome." She winks and then turns to answer the phone. I catch Ben's attention and grin at him when he walks to me as his client takes a rest.

"I'm headed out," I say.

"Listen, I'm so sorry that I'm pulled in a million directions."

"You own a business, Ben. It happens. I'm getting my workouts in, and eating my meals. Everything's fine. In fact, I have to meet the chef at my place in a little bit because he made me meals for the next few days."

"Thanks for letting me give him your number," he replies, looking back at the client. I know he's antsy to get back to it.

"No problem. I'll see you tomorrow."

I wave and turn to leave, already getting a plan in place for later. Our cheat day isn't until tomorrow, but maybe I can start it this evening.

He's been working extra hard, after all.

* * * *

It's almost 9:15 p.m., and Ben should be home. Unless he stayed at the gym to work in his office, but I hope he left.

He lives in a townhouse about thirty minutes from where I'm

staying. Which surprised me. That means he leaves his place at 5:30 in the morning every day just to train me. No wonder the poor man looks so dang tired.

When I pull into the driveway, I'm relieved to see lights on inside. I hope that means he's here, and his SUV is tucked away inside the garage.

I walk to the front door and ring the bell, armed with a box of pizza that smells like heaven.

It only takes about thirty seconds for the door to open, and there he is, standing with the light behind him so he's mostly in silhouette.

"Hey," I say with a smile. "I know it's a day early, but delivery!"

He holds the door open wide and gestures for me to come inside. His place is clean and simple. Pretty much what you'd expect a bachelor pad to look like.

He hasn't said anything, so either he's irritated that I'm here, or he's mad.

Maybe he's mad.

"You don't have to eat it tonight." I turn around. "And I know I should have texted or called. This is dumb. You just looked so tired earlier, and I wanted to do something nice for you. And I admit, I wanted to see you, even if it's only for a minute. But I'll just put this in your fridge and go because you're probably exhausted and super annoyed that I just came over without being invited."

I ramble when I'm nervous, and for some reason, I'm *really* nervous.

He takes the box from me, sets it on a table, and rather than reply, frames my face in his hands and kisses me long and slow. This kiss isn't rushed or frantic like they've been in the past.

No, it's sweet and gentle. And, honestly, just as powerful.

"Thank you," he says at last and kisses my forehead. "It smells delicious, and I've only had a protein bar today. Cheat day can start a couple of hours early this week."

I grin and flip the lid open. "I was hoping you'd say that. Pepperoni?"

"This is my favorite pizza, aside from Nic's."

"I know. I called Nic to ask." I shrug and gesture to the kitchen. "Can I grab plates?"

"Sure, they're above the coffee maker."

I grab the plates and a few napkins and join him at the dining room table. "How are you really?"

"I wasn't this tired when I was in the beginning stages of taking the business over from Rich," he confesses and takes a big bite of pizza. "I can't believe Damon just walked out like that. He was at the gym for a long time. Long before I took over. I didn't fire anyone, I just added more trainers. I guess he didn't like some of my changes. When Lisa told him that I'd added another client to his list, it tipped him over the edge and he just walked out."

"I guess you won't give him a reference."

He shrugs and pops the last bite into his mouth. "I shouldn't be bitching to you. You're my client. Supposedly my *only* client right now."

"I'm your friend, too," I remind him and pull my feet up under me. "And we're not working right now."

He reaches for another slice. "Do you want to stay tonight?"

I blink at him. "That wasn't my intention. I just wanted to feed you, I didn't mean to imply that—"

"You didn't imply anything. I'm just asking because I'm tired and I don't have it in me to beat around the bush."

"I want to hang out for a few, and then I'm going home because you need a good night's sleep."

He sighs and rubs his hand down his face. "One of these days, I'm going to get my hands on you for more than five minutes, Rina."

"I hope so," I say bluntly. "But I'm a patient woman." I look around. "I like your place."

He follows my gaze. "Thanks. It works for now. It's close to the gym and all of the things I like in Seattle. What kind of place do you have in Bend?"

"It's a two-story near a golf course," I reply. "I don't golf, but I like grass. And I don't have to mow it."

He stares at me and then busts up laughing. "That's the funniest thing I've heard all day."

I grin, enjoying the sound of his laughter. "I like it when you smile, Ben. You have a great one."

He watches me from across the table. The chemistry between us is ridiculous. It sparks whenever we're within fifty yards of each other. "Are you sure you don't want to stay?"

"No. But you really do need to rest, and I'll see you in about eight hours."

"Too damn long."

* * * *

"How's everything going up there?" Zane asks two days later. We're chatting on our weekly call, and I'm organizing some of the donations in the upstairs guest bedroom.

"Pretty well, actually. I'm feeling stronger every day. Still sore as fuck, but my clothes are fitting differently. I'm even getting used to eating a lot of kale."

"I hate kale," he says.

"Me, too. I haven't seen a lot of Ben, though. I mean, I see him a couple times a day for training, but not much else."

"And?"

"And I got used to seeing him more often, that's all."

"No, that's not all. Spill it, sugar."

"There's nothing to spill. We've kissed a few times, but that's it."

He's quiet, so I keep talking.

"There would probably be more, but he had a trainer quit on him, so he's been working long hours at the gym. He's got a lot on his plate. But Lisa, his assistant, told me yesterday that he finally hired someone new. They start tomorrow, so that should help lighten Ben's load a bit."

"Yes, by all means, let's lighten Ben's load."

I scowl at the phone sitting next to me. "You're gross."

"So, what's the deal here?"

"There's no deal. I'm attracted to him. Okay, that's an understatement. He's sexy, Zane. Like, sexier than any movie star I've ever seen."

"Thanks."

"And he's kind and supportive. If I can't push a certain weight, he walks me through it, encouraging me until I *can*. And let's be honest--"

"Yes, let's."

"When we're together, the sparks are off the charts."

"So sleep with him, then. What's the problem?"

"He's busy. I told you, I've hardly seen him. And I have to say, I miss him. Is that weird?"

"Probably. But he hired someone, and now he'll have some time on his hands. Fill it with a little fun. Just don't get too attached, because your life isn't in Seattle."

I stare at the donations around me. "Yeah."

"Rina."

"I know, my life's in Bend."

"Then why do you sound like that?"

I blow out a breath and then tell him about my new donation venture here in the Emerald City.

"So maybe your life isn't in Bend anymore," he says in surprise.

"Yes, it is. My house is there, I have friends there, *and* a nonprofit to run."

"Let's continue the honesty here, Mel has the nonprofit covered."

I bite my lip. I'd been thinking the same thing.

"Yeah, I could look in on them every few months, and it would most likely be fine without me." But moving is *huge*, and I'm not quite ready to think that way yet.

"Looks like it's a good thing that I'll be there in a little over a week for Christmas. I need to check out this Ben guy."

"Be nice," I warn him. "I'm serious, Zane, he's a good person."

"I'm always nice."

I snort-laugh. "Right. That's why the tabloids have stories of you making people cry on set."

"Why are you reading the rags, Rina?"

I shrug, even though he can't see me. "Why are you making people cry?"

"I didn't. It was an exaggeration."

"Sure, it was. Well, I'm excited to see you late next week, but you have to promise me you'll behave when you're here."

"No. I'll see you soon. Love you."

He clicks off.

I roll my eyes.

This should be fun.

* * * *

"Isn't this the cutest thing you've ever seen?" Brynna asks as she shows us a baby onesie with pink bunnies all over it. "I miss my girls being this little."

"You could have more babies," Natalie reminds her.

Natalie, Jules, Nic, and Brynna came over this evening to help me get organized to drop all of this off to shelters before the holidays. We're into our third bottle of wine, and I've even had one cupcake.

They've been sworn to secrecy.

"That ship has sailed," Brynna says and sighs.

"How many kids do you have?" I ask her.

"Three," she answers. "Twin girls, who are the teenagers from hell right now, and a little boy in first grade."

"I can't believe he's in the first grade," Jules says. "Also, Stella's only six, and so much has changed in baby stuff since she was tiny."

"It changes constantly," Natalie agrees. "There's more here than I realized."

"I'm going to have to spread it out over a couple of shelters," I agree. "And it's because you guys are awesome."

"We really are." Jules nods and then giggles. "Just kidding."

"No, you *really* are," I stress. "Do you have any idea how much pleading and begging I usually have to do to get donations like this? I can't even tell you how much I appreciate it."

"Hey, I was a single mom for a long time," Brynna says. "Before Caleb came into my life, I was on my own for a couple of years. Now, yes, I have a wonderful family, and I never worried about being on the streets, but money was tight. I remember what that feels like. It's scary, especially when you're trying to take care of your babies. It takes a village, you know?"

A couple of hours later, we finally have everything organized and packed into gift bags of snacks, bags of hygiene products, and baskets of baby goodies.

"I'll leave it up to the shelters to gift the big pieces and the breast pumps to the women they know need them the most."

"You might want to contact a women's clinic for those things,"

Natalie suggests. "They usually know which patients are in need."

"Good idea," I say, making a mental note.

We clean up our mess, toss away the wine bottles, and I make Jules take the cupcakes with her.

"They can't stay here," I insist. "Ben will know I had one if he sees this box."

"You had two," Brynna reminds me.

"Shh." I cover my mouth with my finger. "That's a secret."

"Our rides are here," Natalie announces. "Thanks for the fun evening, Rina."

"Thank *you* for your help."

I wave them off as their men pour the girls into vehicles and drive away. Once they're gone, I close the door and survey the scene.

The wrappings are feminine and fun. Uplifting. We also wrote little notes to go with each one to help boost the person's mood. I don't want the recipients to feel like charity cases.

I want them to feel as if they just got the best present ever.

The doorbell rings, and I turn to open it, sure it's one of the girls picking up something they forgot.

But it's not.

It's Ben.

He swoops in, in that way he does that literally sweeps me off my feet.

The door closes, and I'm immediately pinned against it again, enjoying this strong man as he kisses the hell out of me.

"I owe you an apology," he says as he comes up for air. "I let you down this week, but that ends right now. You officially have my undivided attention again."

"Okay." I swallow hard as I watch his Adam's apple bob in his throat. "Thanks."

"And one more thing."

"What's that?"

"I've missed you." His voice is tender as he drags the pad of his thumb across my lower lip. "I've wanted to kiss you, to *touch* you, so damn bad I ached with it."

"I'm right here," I whisper. That's all the invitation he needs to lift me into his arms and carry me up the stairs to my bedroom.

"Before we take this any further," he says as he lowers me to the bed, "I brought condoms."

"Good, because I don't have any."

"I'm also clean."

"Me, too."

"Great, can we be done with the non-sexy portion of the program now?"

I grin and fist my hand in his shirt, pulling him toward me on the mattress. "Yes, please."

We're a tangle of sighs and limbs as we work our clothes off. When his body is finally free from clothing, I take a second to give him a long look.

"Ben, you look like you were sculpted from marble. I know it takes a lot of work and dedication to look like this, and it's a little intimidating."

"Are you kidding me?" He kisses his way down my shoulder to my arm. "Have you seen yourself, Sabrina? You have curves in all the right places, and the softest skin I've ever touched. I can't get enough of you."

He plants wet kisses down my torso, over my navel, and to the promised land, where he sets up camp for what seems like an hour.

Dear, sweet Moses.

My back arches, and my hands fist in his hair as he takes me on a long journey toward the most explosive orgasm of my life.

And just when I think it can't get any better, he uses one of those condoms he brought with him and covers me, cradling my head in his hands as he fills me completely and stares at me with those intense blue eyes of his.

"Ah, fuck, babe."

His movements are long and slow as if he's trying to draw this out for as long as possible, but I want him to go faster.

Harder.

Before I can tell him so, he seemingly reads my mind. He picks up the pace and growls against my neck, and that's all it takes to send me over the edge once again—and I happily take him with me.

He rolls to the side, still inside me, and works on catching his breath as he traces my nipple with the tip of his finger.

"That was worth waiting for."

"Oh, yeah."

"But I'm not going to wait that long again before I'm inside you."

"Thank God."

Chapter Seven

~Ben~

I haven't been home in a week.

Well, that's not quite true. I went home to get clothes and toiletries and to make sure the roof hadn't caved in, but aside from that, I haven't been there since the first night with Rina.

I wasn't kidding when I told her she'd have my undivided attention. I hired *two* new trainers, one full-time and one part-time, to make sure there were no more incidents like the one that happened when Damon walked out.

Luke's paying me too well to screw this up.

And I enjoy being with Rina.

This morning, just like every morning, we were up and out of bed by five, and out the door for a bike ride by six. I've always enjoyed riding, but it's even better with Rina. She laughs and gets a little goofy, even when I'm pushing her hard and throwing challenging hills in her way.

Once we got back to her place, she went up for a shower, and I started preparing breakfast. She prefers my breakfast burritos, so that's what I'm making, while thinking of her naked and wet upstairs.

I'd like to join her.

But we have a lot on our plate today, and there's no time for that.

Just as I roll the burrito and set it on the plate, her doorbell rings. I wipe my hands on a towel and walk to the door, surprised to find a man grinning back at me.

"Where's Sabrina?" he asks by way of greeting.

"Indisposed. Who's asking?"

He raises an eyebrow. "I'm Zane, and I'm here for the holidays, of course. Where else would I be? I mean the world to her."

My eyes narrow as my stomach turns to lead. Of course, I know who he is. I didn't know Rina was expecting him. "I see. I'll let her know you're here."

I stride away and head up the stairs, straight for the bedroom. There's a guy in her life? Why the fuck didn't she say something?

"Because you're a fool," I mumble as I reach for my duffle and start tossing my shit inside.

"What's going on?" Rina asks as she steps into the room, wrapped in a towel, her hair wet from the shower.

"I'm out of here," I reply without looking at her.

"Why?"

"Your boyfriend is downstairs. Wait, is he your husband?" I stop packing and turn to her. "If you tell me that dude is your husband, we're going to have an even bigger issue here."

"Who?" she asks, scowling. "What the hell is happening?"

"Zane."

She wrinkles her nose. "Ew. No, he's not my boyfriend *or* my husband. He played my brother for years. He's my best friend. And for the record, I don't have a man in my life."

I tip my head to the side, and she sighs in defeat.

"That came out wrong. *You're* the man in my life right now. I don't have another boyfriend, husband, fuck buddy, blah blah blah. I have Zane, and he's my best friend, and shit, he's coming here today."

"Yeah, he's already here."

She covers her mouth and sits on the bed. "Sorry. I forgot to mention it. We always spend Christmas together because both of our families are assholes. You have Nic. I have Zane. So, yeah. He's here. Sorry."

I set my bag on the floor and blow out a breath as she stands and crosses to me.

"I've never been jealous a day in my life."

"If the roles were reversed, I might have scratched someone's eyes out," she admits. "Every time I thought to say something, we weren't together. He'll be here through Christmas day. You'll like him."

"What's not to like?"

We turn at the voice in the doorway.

"You let me believe that you have a claim on her."

He smiles smugly, but his hazel eyes are calculating.

"You're a dick," I add.

"I'm absolutely that," he says. "Come here and give me some sugar, sugar."

"Not until she's dressed," I reply.

"You guys take your macho-man BS downstairs. I'll be there in a minute," Rina says, pushing us both out of the room. "Be nice to each other."

"I'm nice," I mutter as we file downstairs to the kitchen. "Burrito?"

"I'd love one," Zane agrees. "It was an early flight, and I haven't eaten much. So, you're the Ben she's been talking about."

Knowing that Rina's talked about me gives me immense satisfaction.

"I'm Ben," I confirm. "And I hate to burst your bubble, but she hasn't said much about you."

"Not surprising, Rina's always been a private person. We go way back. We were on a show together as kids."

I nod and go to work making another burrito. I've just added egg whites when Rina bounces down the stairs and launches herself into Zane's arms, giving him a tight hug.

I want to punch him.

And that's stupid. I hug Nic. She's *my* best friend.

"I'm *so* happy to see you," Rina says, smiling up at Zane. Of course, I recognize him. Zane is a megastar. I'd have to live in a tiny village in the middle of the Amazon to not know who he is.

It's like not knowing Brad Pitt.

But he currently has his hands on my girl, and friend or not, it makes me twitchy.

"How was your flight?" Rina asks him.

"Not bad," he answers. "It was early enough that I was only recognized a handful of times."

"Why didn't you take a private plane?" I ask him.

"Because I forgot to book it." He shrugs. "I'm always forgetting something."

"You have an assistant for that," Rina reminds him.

"I fired her."

"Why?"

"Because she got naked and climbed into bed with me, and I'm not comfortable with that."

"Ew." Rina wrinkles her nose in disgust. "What is *wrong* with people? And why do you keep hiring young, pretty women?"

"Because I like looking at them, but that doesn't mean I want to fuck them."

"Hire an old married dude with grandkids," Rina suggests. "He won't give two shits about sleeping with you, and will get your planes booked for you."

"That's boring," Zane mutters. "Okay, so Christmas is in four days, and you don't have a tree up. Not one twinkle light or poinsettia in this place. What's wrong with you?"

"We've been a little busy," Rina says. "We don't need a tree to exchange gifts."

"Uh, yeah, we do. We'll go get one today."

"I'm working today," Rina informs him.

"Fine. *I'll* get one today."

"You can take the day," I offer, but she's already shaking her head.

"No way. I'm here to work. Z can party all day with his fancy tree and twinkle lights."

"I'm not sure I like the way that sounds," Zane quips, making us both laugh.

* * * *

"Where's Rina?" Jules asks. I was invited to dinner at Nic and Matt's, and Jules and Nate are here, as well. Matt and Jules are very close. All the Montgomerys are, but I have a feeling Matt and Jules have a special sibling bond.

"She's at home. With Zane."

Four pairs of eyes turn to me.

"Who the fuck is Zane?" Nate asks.

"Wait," Nic says, holding up a hand. "Is it Zane Cooper, the movie star?"

"One and the same."

"Wow," Nic breathes, earning a look from her husband. "If Matt were to ever give me a hall pass—and trust me, we all know that's never gonna happen—"

"Walking a fine line here, little one."

"Zane would be mine. My hall pass. Whoa."

"He's a hottie," Jules agrees, and now it's Nate's turn to narrow his gaze on his wife.

This is entertaining as hell.

"Why is he with Rina?" Matt asks.

"He showed up this morning. I guess they're best friends and always spend the holidays together."

"Seriously?" Nic asks. "I wonder if she'd introduce me to him."

Matt's staring at Nic now, tugging his lower lip thoughtfully. "Yes, I wonder if she would."

Nic's face flushes in embarrassment. "I mean, I know that's silly. Never mind."

"I think Nic might be getting spanked later." Jules giggles.

"Oh, she will be, yes," Matt replies, still watching his wife. "Among other things."

"That's cool that she has someone here with her for the holidays," Jules says. "Of course, you're both welcome to join us for Christmas dinner. It's loud and chaotic, and the kids will be running amok, most likely high on sugar and playing with loud toys, but you're welcome to join us."

"That's so...*not* tempting." I laugh. "But thank you for the offer."

"How are things going with her?" Nate asks as he adds more salad to his plate. "How's the training?"

"She's a trooper," I reply. "She doesn't complain about any of it, even when I know she's got to be incredibly sore. She's up early, ready to go by six, and there are days we're not finished until six in the evening."

"Jesus, you make her work out for twelve hours?" Nic asks, scowling at me. "That can't be legal."

"Not for twelve hours straight," I say. "But there is a lot of different interval training involved, along with stretching and yoga, meals, that sort of thing. I take up a good portion of her day."

"And what about the rest of it?" Matt asks.

"What do you mean?"

He tilts his head. "I see the way you look at her. I hear your voice when you speak about her. This is more than a working relationship."

"Wait, what?" Nic demands. "Why didn't you tell me?"

"We're compatible in a lot of ways." I choose my words carefully.

"Benjamin Demarco, you're falling in love with her." Nic gasps.

I lick my lips and nod, not denying it. "Yeah, it seems I am. Who would've thought, right?"

"How does she feel?" Jules asks.

"You'd have to ask her," I say. "We've only been sleeping together for a week. I barely know her. But she's great. And when I thought that Zane was here *for* her this morning, well… Let's just say I had a bad moment."

"Did you punch him?" Nate asks.

"I wanted to, but I might've killed him, and I can't be with Rina from jail."

"I like her," Nic says. "I like her a lot."

I nod and steer the conversation away from my personal life. Because the truth is, I've fallen hard and fast for an incredible woman, but I don't know what's going to happen in a few short weeks when our working relationship is over.

And it's something I'm not ready to think about.

* * * *

Going home alone after a week of spending my nights with Rina isn't ideal, but I'm not going to crash the Zane and Rina Christmas party tonight. They haven't seen each other in a long time, and I don't need to be attached to her at the hip while they talk and catch up.

I do, however, miss her.

But it's fine. I'll go home and do some work in my office before I turn in early.

I pull into my garage and frown when I walk inside and find lights on.

I know I didn't leave any on when I was here three days ago.

Is someone squatting in my house?

I hurry through the place, but I don't see anyone. I climb the stairs and rush into my bedroom, then come to an abrupt halt when I find Rina in my bed, under the covers. She grins when she sees me and reveals one long, sculpted leg, her toes pointed against the white sheets.

I've never been so relieved to see anyone in my life. My mood lifts instantly, and my cock twitches in my jeans.

"So, I got an idea earlier when Zane told the story about his assistant climbing into bed with him naked."

"Yeah? Tell me."

"I thought it would be fun if I was here, waiting for you. Naked."

She lets the covers fall, revealing her perfect breasts.

"That is an excellent idea. How did you get in here?"

She bites her lip. "Don't waste time with stupid questions. Take those clothes off."

"Yes, ma'am."

Chapter Eight

~Sabrina~

"Who wants more egg rolls?" I ask as I return to the living room carrying the takeout boxes of Chinese food. Zane and I always order Chinese on Christmas Eve.

It's tradition.

"Duh," Zane says, reaching to pluck them off the platter.

"I like the decorations." Ben looks around as he uses his chopsticks to eat his stir-fry. While Zane and I both got breaded, sweet and sour everything, Ben stuck to chicken and veggies.

Because he's healthy.

But it's Christmas, and I'm splurging a little.

"Zane did a good job," I say. "I was shocked."

"How dare you?" Zane asks.

"Dude, you're a superstar actor, not an interior decorator."

My best friend shrugs. "I can be both. Also, I might have called someone to make this happen."

"That close to Christmas?" Ben asks before I can.

"I paid extra." Zane grins and reaches under the tree for a present and passes it to me. "Okay, one gift tonight. That's how we always do it."

"Yay! It's my favorite part." I tear into the red and gold paper, letting it fall to the floor at my feet. "Thank you. I needed new earbuds for the gym."

"They're wireless," Zane says proudly. "And you're welcome."

We keep exchanging gifts, and Ben opens a pair of riding gloves I got him for his bike, and Zane the cashmere scarf I bought online.

Then we settle in with a glass of wine and enjoy the glow of the lights on the tree.

"So, why is it that neither of you likes to spend the holidays with your families?" Ben asks. He links his fingers with mine and kisses the back of my hand.

"Most people who were child actors have a strained relationship with their parents," I reply.

"And ours did what they all do," Zane continues. "They took control of our careers and our money while we worked our asses off. They sold us to the highest bidder to pad their bank accounts."

"But it's your money." Ben frowns.

"Technically, but as minors, our parents had power of attorney. So, they had control of every penny. My parents started selling personal photos for the rags when we were about twelve."

Zane's eyes find mine.

"That's fucked up," Ben says.

"They liked feeding the rumor that Rina and I were an item," Zane replies. "And the rags ate that shit right up. So, as the years went on, Rina and I tried to keep our friendship on the down low so we could have some sort of normal relationship."

"The rumors came and went over the years, and people speculated if we were together." I shrug and sip my wine. "We haven't been photographed together in ages. Aside from selfies that we keep for ourselves, anyway. When I decided to leave the business because I was sick and hungry *all the time*, my parents were pissed. I was pulling the plug on their cushy way of life. In other words, they'd have to get real jobs. I barely speak to them now."

"I'm sorry," Ben says. "That's pretty shitty."

"My parents divorced when I was young, mostly because they couldn't agree on how to spend the money I made, and they fought like cats and dogs. They each remarried, several times," Zane says, "and had more kids. And I got lost somewhere in the shuffle. Not that

I'm super bummed, given they're both assholes."

"And now you have each other." Ben smiles.

"Yeah, he's stuck with me," I reply and grin at my best friend. "What about you, Ben? Are you close to your family?"

"My parents died a few years ago, and I was an only child, so I don't have a lot of family. Nic's pretty much it."

"So, we're the three misfits," I say.

"Speak for yourself," Zane argues. "I'm no misfit."

* * * *

"Why did you wear a necklace to the gym?" Zane asks me the next morning. We're at Sound Fitness, working on weights, and I'm toying with the sweetheart necklace Ben gave me this morning. It came in a Tiffany blue box, which pretty much made my year.

"Because it was a gift, and I want to wear it."

Zane shakes his head and laughs at me before reclining on the bench press. Out of the corner of my eye, I see Ben walking away, heading toward the front desk.

He said yesterday that he closes the gym down by noon on Christmas day, staying open just long enough for the diehards to get a workout in first thing in the morning.

I glance behind me, but when Ben turns to say something to Lisa at the desk, I realize it's not Ben at all.

Some of the trainers are in, working with a few clients, but just as I suspected on Christmas morning, it's quiet here, which puts Zane at ease.

The poor man is always accosted by someone wanting a photo.

"Look," someone says, pointing outside.

"Snow," someone else says.

"Well, that'll shut the city down for a week," Lisa grumbles.

"Aww, isn't that sweet?" I turn to Zane. "You get a white Christmas."

"Adorable," he agrees. Zane always tries to seem cocky, so *tough*, but that's just his defense mechanism. I know he makes it sound as if he's better off without his parents, but he carries a lot of hurt from that whole situation. "I'll be able to use the awesome scarf you got me."

"Absolutely."

Once we've finished our workout, I go on the hunt for Ben. He's been roaming around, checking in on people and then hiding away in his office again. I know he's giving me space to spend time with Zane, and I appreciate it, but I only have a little time left in Seattle, and I want to spend time with Ben, as well.

"Knock-knock." I lean on the doorframe to his office. "We're done."

"I'm about finished, too," he says. "The others can handle things here until noon, and then they'll all go home. I'd like to take you somewhere, just the two of us."

"I'm game for that."

Ben drove here early this morning, and I rode in with Zane an hour ago or so. I find my friend and let him know that I'll see him a little later.

"I'm gonna go nap." Zane yawns. "And then eat leftovers."

"Save some for me." I wave him off and turn to find a woman scowling at me. I don't intend to engage with her, but before I can turn away, she props her hands on her hips and starts spewing words at me.

"You should be ashamed of yourself. You're leading *two* men on at the same time."

"I have no idea what you're talking about."

I turn to walk away, and she keeps talking. Loudly.

"It's not fair to treat Ben like that. He's a nice guy. You're nothing but a stupid bitch, treating people like that."

I turn and raise a brow at Lisa, who immediately jumps into action, but Ben's already there.

"We don't allow that kind of behavior in my gym. You can go. And don't come back."

She gasps and clutches her chest. "I'm just defending *you*."

"And I don't need it. Go." When the woman slams out the front door, Ben turns to Lisa. "I don't know who that is, but cancel her membership and refund her money. She's done."

"You got it," Lisa says, already typing on the computer.

"Come on." Ben holds out his hand for mine. "Let's get out of here. Merry Christmas, Lisa."

"Merry Christmas, guys!"

We climb into Ben's SUV and pull out of the parking lot, and I still haven't said anything.

"Is that how I act?" I ask aloud. "I don't think I flirt with Zane."

"You don't," he assures me. "Whoever that chick is, she's jealous."

"I suppose." I stare out the window and watch big flakes fall to the ground. "Will this snowfall really shut the city down?"

"If it sticks, it will. It's not cold enough right now to freeze, but it could overnight. Seattle isn't exactly equipped to deal with harsh weather. I don't really have anywhere specific I want to take you. I just wanted some alone time with you."

"Well, that doesn't hurt my feelings." I smile over at him. "I know Zane being here sort of threw a wrench in things, but in my defense, when we agreed that he'd come for Christmas, I didn't know that you and I would, well, do whatever it is we're doing."

He grins. "It's fine. I like him."

"Me, too."

My phone pings in my pocket, so I pull it out and see a text from Melanie. Expecting a Merry Christmas, I open it and scowl in disbelief.

Mel: *Are you and Zane together? Like, a couple?*

I shake my head and type a reply.

Me: *You know better than that. Of course not.*

A sinking feeling sets up residence in my belly as I watch the three dots bounce as Mel types her reply.

All she sends is a link.

I click on it, and a website appears with the headline *Zane and Sabrina: Reunited!*

I briefly skim the article, which goes on to say that Zane and I are cuddled up in Seattle, secretly engaging in a torrid affair. That the rumors from all of these years must be true.

"Take me home," I say immediately.

"What's wrong?"

I'm staring at the photos. Zane and I are in the gym, just this morning, laughing and talking. In one shot, he takes my hand and helps me up off the floor, and then I'm leaning against him, laughing at something he just said.

It looks intimate.

Something at the side of the photo catches my eye.

"Rina? What is it?"

I enlarge the photo and feel my blood run cold. It's Ben, from behind, on the other side of a wall that separates that part of the gym from the reception area. A woman has her arms around him, her fingers in his hair, and he's kissing her passionately.

What in the actual fuck? The thoughts in my head swirl, and my heart hurts. I just want to go home and *hide*.

"Rina."

"It seems someone enjoyed taking a lot of photos at the gym this morning," I say at last and flash the screen at him, with the headline showing. "Zane and I being together is all over social media. Mel sent this to me."

"That was literally an hour ago."

"Word spreads fast in the age of technology," I remind him. "I'm such an idiot. Zane's going to be so pissed."

"This isn't your fault," Ben says.

"Actually, you're right." I turn in my seat to face him. "It's *your* fault. How could you let this happen, Ben? We were supposed to be safe in your gym."

His gaze bounces up to the rearview mirror, and he curses.

"This car behind me has been on my ass since we left the gym."

I glance back, but I don't recognize the driver.

"It could be a paparazzo."

Ben shakes his head. "There's no way they could get here that fast."

"You have no idea what they're capable of," I murmur and sit back, silent as Ben turns into my driveway.

I hurry out of the car and see a man jump out of the vehicle that was following us.

"Sabrina!" he yells. "Can you confirm that you and Zane are getting married?"

"What is wrong with you?" I demand, turning to the reporter. "Of course, we aren't. We've been friends for more than twenty goddamn years, you piece of shit."

"Get out of here before I call the cops," Ben growls and leads me to the door. When we're safely inside, and Ben has locked the deadbolt behind us, I round on him.

"This is fucked up, Ben."

"Agreed."

"What's going on?"

Chapter Nine

~Ben~

Zane comes hurrying down the stairs. "Why are you yelling?"

"You're not going to like this," Rina says but taps on the screen of her phone, then passes it over to him. "Security breach at the gym."

I'm totally calm on the outside, but inside, I'm seething mad. I want to know who the fuck did this, and I want to know *now*. But before I charge back into work to get some answers, I need to make things right with Rina first.

"Fuck," Zane says, dragging his hand down his face. "Well, who gives a shit, sugar? Let them talk. If they're talking about us, they're leaving someone else alone."

"We worked hard for *years* to not have this happen," she replies. She looks as if she's on the verge of tears, and I want to pull her to me and assure her that I'll fix this.

But I have no idea *how* to fix it.

"My staff wouldn't do this," I begin, and Rina turns to me.

"Well, *someone* did. And you might not think it's a big deal, but you're wrong. It's a big fucking deal, Ben. And you know what? I don't want to talk to you right now. You should go."

I stand, stunned. "You're kicking me out?"

"Yes. I am. Please go."

She hurries up the stairs and slams her bedroom door. Zane shrugs.

"This will blow over," he says. "Give her a couple of hours to calm down. She can't stay mad for long."

"I don't blame her for being pissed," I reply. "I'm surprised you don't want to punch me in the face."

"I do." Zane grins. "But that won't help anything. Looks like I have some calls to make. I'll lock up behind you."

That's my not-so-subtle hint to leave, so I walk out to my car, ignoring the asshole still staked out in front of the house, and do the only thing I can think of.

I call Luke.

"Hey, Ben, Merry Christmas."

"Hi, Luke. There's an issue."

As I drive back toward the gym, I fill him in on the situation. "I'm on my way back now to chew some asses and figure out how this happened. But now I don't know what to do about the paparazzo sitting in front of your house."

"I'll handle that," he says, but there's an edge to his voice that tells me he's pissed. "My wife and I have worked hard to keep our family out of the spotlight, Ben. Part of that is keeping that house under the radar. We've had other superstars stay there without even a whisper in the press."

And now I've fucked all of that up.

"I'm sorry. This is not how I operate."

"That's why I hired you. But now I have to clean up a goddamn mess on Christmas day."

He hangs up, and I cringe. I pull into the parking lot, cut the engine, and run inside. My staff is just getting ready to go home.

"My office. Now. All of you."

I can feel them looking at each other as I stomp through the gym to my office and stand behind my desk. Lisa and the four trainers join me, all looking nervous.

"Photos were taken today that got leaked to the fucking tabloids," I inform them. "Zane's and Sabrina's privacy was invaded, and now my reputation is at stake. If any of you knows anything about this, you'd better speak up right effing now."

Lisa immediately starts tapping on her phone, her face pulled into a frown. A newer trainer, Bonnie, raises her hand.

"I was working with a woman this morning. I stepped away from her to check on another client, and when I returned, I noticed she was taking pictures. I told her right away that she needed to delete them, and she promised she would."

"Well, she didn't," I reply, my voice full of ice. "And now Rina's not speaking to me, and Luke Williams, my *boss,* is fucking pissed."

"I'm not sure if Rina isn't speaking to you just because of her photo being taken," Lisa says as she approaches me, looking at her phone. "It could have something to do with you making out with another chick."

She shows me the picture, and I scowl. "I didn't make out with anyone."

"It looks like you," Lisa points out. "And you're sucking that girl's face right off."

"It's not me," I say again, this time with a growl.

"I think it's me." Aiden, the newest trainer, clears his throat. "My girlfriend stopped by because it's Christmas, and I, uh, kissed the hell out of her."

"You two look alike from behind," Lisa interjects. "I get you confused all the time."

"Damn it." I pace the floor behind my desk. "Okay, first thing we're going to do is this. Effective immediately, there are to be no cell phones on the floor. They have to be left in lockers. That's non-negotiable. I could lose my business over this.

"And second," I continue, "no kissing the hell out of someone while you're at work. I get that it's Christmas, and it sucks to be here today, but it's not professional, no matter what day it is."

"I agree," Aiden says and nods. "It won't happen again. I apologize."

"Okay, now I have to go convince Rina that I'm not an asshole."

"Good luck," Lisa calls after me.

* * * *

I hurry to Rina's place and breathe a sigh of relief when I pull into the drive and see that the paparazzo is gone.

Luke handled it fast.

I knock on the door and wait, but there's no answer. I bang on it again.

Zane pulls it open and says, "She doesn't want to see you right now."

"Too bad. Let me the fuck in, Zane."

"Normally, I'd stay out of things like this because, at the end of the day, it's not any of my business. Except, this time, it is. Because it's Rina, and she told me to keep you out of here for the time being. I told you, she won't stay mad forever. You could try back tomorrow morning."

"I want to see her *now*."

"And I just told you, she doesn't want to see *you* right now." Zane's expression is sober, and I know I'm in for a fight.

I don't fucking care. I'll do whatever I have to do to make things right.

"I'm coming inside."

"Come on, man," Zane says with a sigh. "A few hours won't matter. Just come back later."

"Oh, for Pete's sake." Sabrina pushes Zane out of the way and glares at me. "What?"

"Let me in."

Chapter Ten

~Ben~

"Honestly, Zane's right. I need a little time to calm down, Ben."

"No, because I have a feeling you're mad about something that you shouldn't be."

She steps back, and I walk inside, but she moves away from me, headed for the kitchen.

"You know, I understand that shit happens. And that because of the celebrity that Zane and I have, there are no guarantees that our privacy is secure. But we were supposed to be safe with *you*."

That's a stab to the heart. "You are. I've already addressed the security issue at the gym. I'm sorry it happened this time, but it won't ever happen again. You have my word."

"And about the other thing, I'm still *here*," she says. "I'm not even out of town yet, and you're already making out with some new girl. And I was only twenty yards away! I mean, who the fuck does that, Ben?"

"That wasn't me."

"I'm not stupid."

Zane snorts from the other room, earning a glare from Rina. "Shut up in there!"

"You know what? Fuck this." I take her hand and lead her up the stairs to her bedroom and shut the door, locking it from the inside. "I'm not going to have this conversation with Zane listening in. That is *not* me kissing that woman. It's Aiden."

"Who the hell is Aiden?"

"One of my new trainers," I reply. "Lisa thinks we look the same from behind."

Recognition dawns in her eyes, and I feel my stomach start to loosen.

"Rina, I've been with you for *weeks*. And I don't know if you missed it, but I've been too busy trying to get my hands on you to notice anyone else. Jesus, I've fallen in love with you."

"Wait, what?" Her eyes are wide as she stands in the middle of the room, soaking in my words.

"I know it's fast, and it sounds completely and certifiably crazy, but I'm in love with you, Rina. I don't want to kiss or do anything else with another person. Only you."

The corners of her lips tip up. "Really?"

"Really." I walk to her and push my fingers through her soft hair. "I'm so sorry that you saw that and assumed the worst."

"It was pretty horrible," she admits and swallows hard. "I mean, I've known from the beginning that this isn't going to last forever, but—"

"We don't know how long anything is going to last," I interrupt and softly kiss her plump lips. "But I can tell you, right here right now, that you're the only woman for me, Sabrina. Without a doubt in my mind."

I lead her over to the bed and take my time undressing her, nibbling on her and glorying in her soft sighs. Her neck arches, and I lick her skin, right where her pulse thrums in her throat.

Her hands tighten on me. I know her neck is a sensitive spot, so I hang out there as my hands roam over her delectable little body.

The brush of my thumb over her nipple earns me a little moan. And when my hand drifts down her belly to her wet core, she gasps.

"Everything right here, from these sweet noises of yours to your warm skin, is mine, Sabrina. Do you get that?"

"Oh, yeah." She raises her hips, inviting my fingers inside of her, and I oblige, almost coming undone when her pussy tightens around me like a fucking vise. I can't get enough of watching her, whether it be when she's laughing or working out, or giving in to her pleasure when we're like this.

She's absolutely incredible.

And she'll never question again whether I'm devoted to her or not. I'll make damn sure of that.

"Look at me, baby." She opens her eyes and watches me as she climbs that hill and then goes over the other side into pure ecstasy. "That's right. Go over, my love."

She shivers and then moans, and I can't hold back any longer. I protect us both and slide home, inside this beautiful woman. This is exactly where I'm supposed to be.

The ride is long and slow, and when we're nothing more than a tangled mess of sweaty limbs and gasping breaths, Rina brushes her fingers through my hair and kisses my cheek.

"I love you, too, you know."

My head comes up, and I stare down at her. "Yeah?"

"Yeah. And I don't care that it's fast. I don't care what anyone else thinks. Sometimes life just happens, and you meet someone you recognize. Someone that always held a place in your life, you just never knew it before."

I kiss her forehead and then her nose. "You have a way with words, babe."

"And no one else even wrote them for me."

Epilogue

~Ben~

One year later…

"Have you done it yet?" Nic asks. We're at a New Year's Eve party at the O'Callaghan Museum of Glass near Seattle. The entire Montgomery family is here, along with their cousins and extended family. It's a packed party.

"Not yet." I don't usually drink, but I take a sip of champagne to help calm my nerves. "I need to talk to Zane first."

"Well, get a move on. We're only thirty minutes from midnight."

She walks away, and I hunt down Zane. He's sitting near the bar, chatting with Kane O'Callaghan, the artist himself.

"Can I please have a word, Zane?" I ask.

"I need to find my wife," Kane says, then nods and leaves me with Zane.

"What's up?" he asks.

"I've been trying to think of how to approach you about this for weeks, and I think I just have to be blunt about it."

"If you're breaking up with Rina, I'll kill you and make it look like an accident."

I grin at the fierce loyalty in his voice. And I don't doubt for a minute that he could do exactly that.

"No. The opposite, actually. I want to ask her to marry me."

He narrows his eyes on me. "You don't need my permission to do that."

"Actually, yeah, I do. You're her only family, and the *other* man in her life. You know her better than anyone, and she loves you. So, I want your permission to ask her to be my wife."

Zane sighs and looks as emotional as I've ever seen the other man.

"Rina is the best of us," he says. "She deserves so much out of life. More than she realizes. And if you recognize that and want to give it to her, you have my blessing to marry her."

"Thank you." I pat his shoulder, already searching the crowd for the woman I love. "That means a lot, Zane."

"If you're planning to do it at midnight, you'd better get a move on." He grins.

I push my hand into my pocket as I walk away from him, fingering the diamond ring that's been burning a hole there for two months. I was going to propose at the premiere of the movie, but that didn't seem appropriate. I considered doing it the night she officially moved in with me here in Seattle.

But then my hot water heater blew up, and the moment was lost.

And so here, while surrounded by the people we love, I want to ask the woman who means the most to me if she'll spend the rest of her life with me.

I find Rina chatting and giggling with Natalie and Jules. Her eyes light up when she sees me approaching.

I nod at the other ladies, and they quickly move away as if they can sense that something's about to happen.

I've never been more nervous in my life.

"Let's dance." I hold out my hand. She immediately accepts it, and I lead her out onto the dance floor.

The song is soft and slow, perfect for what I have in mind.

"This is a great party," she says as she leans her head on my chest.

"Yeah. You look amazing in this dress."

She smiles up at me. "Thanks. And you're quite dashing in a tux. How is it possible that even with this jacket on, I can still see the outline of your muscles?"

I laugh and lean in to kiss her cheek. "I love you."

"I love you, too."

"I need to talk to you about something serious."

She frowns up at me. "Okay. Me, too. You first."

I tilt my head to the side, curious about what she has to say, but I'm too nervous to stop now. "I don't ever want to spend a day without you, babe. You're the best part of my life."

We stop dancing, and I lower myself to one knee, holding her hand.

"Will you marry me?"

Her eyes flood with unshed tears, and she nods excitedly. I push the ring onto her finger and stand to pull her into my arms. The room erupts into applause, and suddenly, everyone is counting down to the New Year.

"*HAPPY NEW YEAR!*"

I lean in and press my lips to her ear. "You've just made me the happiest man alive."

She shakes her head, surprising me. "I'm hoping that in nine months, you'll be even happier."

I frown, not understanding, but then the light bulb comes on, and I gawk down at her.

"Are you…?"

"Found out this morning," she says and covers her belly with my hand. "So, we might want to get a move on with this wedding."

I whoop and pull her into my arms, spinning her in a circle before kissing the hell out of her.

I'm going to spend the rest of my life with her. And we'll start a new family together. A family that we both need.

* * * *

Also from 1001 Dark Nights and Kristen Proby, discover Wonder With Me, Soaring With Fallon, Tempting Brooke, No Reservations, Easy With You, and Easy For Keeps.

Sign up for the 1001 Dark Nights Newsletter
and be entered to win a Tiffany Key necklace.

There's a contest every month!

Go to www.1001DarkNights.com to subscribe.

**As a bonus, all subscribers can download
FIVE FREE exclusive books!**

Discover 1001 Dark Nights Collection Seven

THE BISHOP by Skye Warren
A Tanglewood Novella

TAKEN WITH YOU by Carrie Ann Ryan
A Fractured Connections Novella

DRAGON LOST by Donna Grant
A Dark Kings Novella

SEXY LOVE by Carly Phillips
A Sexy Series Novella

PROVOKE by Rachel Van Dyken
A Seaside Pictures Novella

RAFE by Sawyer Bennett
An Arizona Vengeance Novella

THE NAUGHTY PRINCESS by Claire Contreras
A Sexy Royals Novella

THE GRAVEYARD SHIFT by Darynda Jones
A Charley Davidson Novella

CHARMED by Lexi Blake
A Masters and Mercenaries Novella

SACRIFICE OF DARKNESS by Alexandra Ivy
A Guardians of Eternity Novella

THE QUEEN by Jen Armentrout
A Wicked Novella

BEGIN AGAIN by Jennifer Probst
A Stay Novella

VIXEN by Rebecca Zanetti
A Dark Protectors/Rebels Novella

SLASH by Laurelin Paige
A Slay Series Novella

THE DEAD HEAT OF SUMMER by Heather Graham
A Krewe of Hunters Novella

WILD FIRE by Kristen Ashley
A Chaos Novella

MORE THAN PROTECT YOU by Shayla Black
A More Than Words Novella

LOVE SONG by Kylie Scott
A Stage Dive Novella

CHERISH ME by J. Kenner
A Stark Ever After Novella

SHINE WITH ME by Kristen Proby
A With Me in Seattle Novella

And new from Blue Box Press:

TEASE ME by J. Kenner
A Stark International Novel

FROM BLOOD AND ASH by Jennifer L. Armentrout
A Blood and Ash Novel

QUEEN MOVE by Kennedy Ryan

THE HOUSE OF LONG AGO by Steve Berry and MJ Rose
A Cassiopeia Vitt Adventure

THE BUTTERFLY ROOM by Lucinda Riley

A KINGDOM OF FLESH AND FIRE by Jennifer L. Armentrout
A Blood and Ash Novel

About Kristen Proby

New York Times and *USA Today* bestselling author Kristen Proby has published more than fifty romance novels. She is best known for her self-published With Me In Seattle and Boudreaux series. Kristen lives in Montana with her husband, two cats, and a spoiled dog.

Discover More Kristen Proby

Wonder With Me: With Me In Seattle Novella

Reed Taylor doesn't pay much attention to the holidays—until he receives a surprise present. Four-year-old Piper is the daughter he never knew about, and with the death of her mother, is also now the roommate he never expected. He's determined to make their first Christmas together one she'll never forget.

Noel Thompson has gotten her share of strange requests in her career as an interior designer. The call to design a beautiful home for Christmas is more like a dream come true. And that was *before* she met her new employer—sexy and mysterious, he's everything she ever hoped Santa would bring her.

As Noel showers his home with holiday spirit, Reed showers Piper with love. And the busy life he's created for himself no longer seems nearly as important as the one Noel is helping him build with his daughter. But if he can't convince his decorator to stay, this could be the only year he feels the true wonder of the season.

* * * *

Tempting Brooke: A Big Sky Novella

Brooke's Blooms has taken Cunningham Falls by surprise. The beautiful, innovative flower shop is trendy, with not only gorgeous flower arrangements, but also fun gifts for any occasion. This store is Brooke Henderson's deepest joy, and it means everything to her, which shows in how completely she and her little shop have been embraced by the small community of Cunningham Falls.

So, when her landlord dies and Brody Chabot saunters through her door, announcing that the building has been sold, and will soon be demolished, Brooke knows that she's in for the fight of her life. But she hasn't gotten this far by sitting back and quietly doing what she's told. *Hustle* is Brooke's middle name, and she has no intention of losing this fight, no matter how tempting Brody's smile -- and body -- is.

* * * *

No Reservations: A Fusion Novella

Chase MacKenzie is *not* the man for Maura Jenkins. A self-proclaimed life-long bachelor, and unapologetic about his distaste for monogamy, a woman would have to be a masochist to want to fall into Chase's bed.

And Maura is no masochist.

Chase has one strict rule: no strings attached. Which is fine with Maura because she doesn't even really *like* Chase. He's arrogant, cocky, and let's not forget bossy. But when he aims that crooked grin at her, she goes weak in the knees. Not that she has any intentions of falling for his charms.

Definitely not.

Well, maybe just once...

* * * *

Easy For Keeps: A Boudreaux Novella

Adam Spencer loves women. All women. Every shape and size, regardless of hair or eye color, religion or race, he simply enjoys them all. Meeting more than his fair share as the manager and head bartender of The Odyssey, a hot spot in the heart of New Orleans' French Quarter, Adam's comfortable with his lifestyle, and sees no reason to change it. A wife and kids, plus the white picket fence are not in the cards for this confirmed bachelor. Until a beautiful woman, and her sweet princess, literally knock him on his ass.

Sarah Cox has just moved to New Orleans, having accepted a position as a social worker specializing in at-risk women and children. It's a demanding, sometimes dangerous job, but Sarah is no shy wallflower. She can handle just about anything that comes at her, even the attentions of one sexy Adam Spencer. Just because he's charmed her daughter, making her think of magical kingdoms with happily ever after, doesn't mean that Sarah believes in fairy tales. But the more time she spends with the enchanting man, the more he begins to sway her into believing in forever.

Even so, when Sarah's job becomes more dangerous than any of them bargained for, will she be ripped from Adam's life forever?

* * * *

Easy With You: A With You In Seattle Novella

Nothing has ever come easy for Lila Bailey. She's fought for every good thing in her life during every day of her thirty-one years. Aside from that one night with an impossible to deny stranger a year ago, Lila is the epitome of responsible.

Steadfast. Strong.

She's pulled herself out of the train wreck of her childhood, proud to be a professor at Tulane University and laying down roots in a city she's grown to love. But when some of her female students are viciously murdered, Lila's shaken to the core and unsure of whom she can trust in New Orleans. When the police detective assigned to the murder case comes to investigate, she's even more surprised to find herself staring into the eyes of the man that made her toes curl last year.

In an attempt to move on from the tragic loss of his wife, Asher Smith moved his daughter and himself to a new city, ready for a fresh start. A damn fine police lieutenant, but new to the New Orleans force, Asher has a lot to prove to his colleagues and himself.

With a murderer terrorizing the Tulane University campus, Asher finds himself toe-to-toe with the one woman that haunts his dreams.

His hands, his lips, his body know her as intimately as he's ever known anyone. As he learns her mind and heart as well, Asher wants nothing more than to keep her safe, in his bed, and in his and his daughter's lives for the long haul.

But when Lila becomes the target, can Asher save her in time, or will he lose another woman he loves?

Discover 1001 Dark Nights

COLLECTION THREE
HIDDEN INK by Carrie Ann Ryan
BLOOD ON THE BAYOU by Heather Graham
SEARCHING FOR MINE by Jennifer Probst
DANCE OF DESIRE by Christopher Rice
ROUGH RHYTHM by Tessa Bailey
DEVOTED by Lexi Blake
Z by Larissa Ione
FALLING UNDER YOU by Laurelin Paige
EASY FOR KEEPS by Kristen Proby
UNCHAINED by Elisabeth Naughton
HARD TO SERVE by Laura Kaye
DRAGON FEVER by Donna Grant
KAYDEN/SIMON by Alexandra Ivy/Laura Wright
STRUNG UP by Lorelei James
MIDNIGHT UNTAMED by Lara Adrian
TRICKED by Rebecca Zanetti
DIRTY WICKED by Shayla Black
THE ONLY ONE by Lauren Blakely
SWEET SURRENDER by Liliana Hart

COLLECTION FOUR
ROCK CHICK REAWAKENING by Kristen Ashley
ADORING INK by Carrie Ann Ryan
SWEET RIVALRY by K. Bromberg
SHADE'S LADY by Joanna Wylde
RAZR by Larissa Ione
ARRANGED by Lexi Blake
TANGLED by Rebecca Zanetti
HOLD ME by J. Kenner
SOMEHOW, SOME WAY by Jennifer Probst
TOO CLOSE TO CALL by Tessa Bailey
HUNTED by Elisabeth Naughton
EYES ON YOU by Laura Kaye
BLADE by Alexandra Ivy/Laura Wright
DRAGON BURN by Donna Grant
TRIPPED OUT by Lorelei James
STUD FINDER by Lauren Blakely

MIDNIGHT UNLEASHED by Lara Adrian
HALLOW BE THE HAUNT by Heather Graham
DIRTY FILTHY FIX by Laurelin Paige
THE BED MATE by Kendall Ryan
NIGHT GAMES by CD Reiss
NO RESERVATIONS by Kristen Proby
DAWN OF SURRENDER by Liliana Hart

COLLECTION FIVE
BLAZE ERUPTING by Rebecca Zanetti
ROUGH RIDE by Kristen Ashley
HAWKYN by Larissa Ione
RIDE DIRTY by Laura Kaye
ROME'S CHANCE by Joanna Wylde
THE MARRIAGE ARRANGEMENT by Jennifer Probst
SURRENDER by Elisabeth Naughton
INKED NIGHTS by Carrie Ann Ryan
ENVY by Rachel Van Dyken
PROTECTED by Lexi Blake
THE PRINCE by Jennifer L. Armentrout
PLEASE ME by J. Kenner
WOUND TIGHT by Lorelei James
STRONG by Kylie Scott
DRAGON NIGHT by Donna Grant
TEMPTING BROOKE by Kristen Proby
HAUNTED BE THE HOLIDAYS by Heather Graham
CONTROL by K. Bromberg
HUNKY HEARTBREAKER by Kendall Ryan
THE DARKEST CAPTIVE by Gena Showalter

COLLECTION SIX
DRAGON CLAIMED by Donna Grant
ASHES TO INK by Carrie Ann Ryan
ENSNARED by Elisabeth Naughton
EVERMORE by Corinne Michaels
VENGEANCE by Rebecca Zanetti
ELI'S TRIUMPH by Joanna Wylde
CIPHER by Larissa Ione

RESCUING MACIE by Susan Stoker
ENCHANTED by Lexi Blake
TAKE THE BRIDE by Carly Phillips
INDULGE ME by J. Kenner
THE KING by Jennifer L. Armentrout
QUIET MAN by Kristen Ashley
ABANDON by Rachel Van Dyken
THE OPEN DOOR by Laurelin Paige
CLOSER by Kylie Scott
SOMETHING JUST LIKE THIS by Jennifer Probst
BLOOD NIGHT by Heather Graham
TWIST OF FATE by Jill Shalvis
MORE THAN PLEASURE YOU by Shayla Black
WONDER WITH ME by Kristen Proby
THE DARKEST ASSASSIN by Gena Showalter

Discover Blue Box Press

TAME ME by J. Kenner
TEMPT ME by J. Kenner
DAMIEN by J. Kenner
TEASE ME by J. Kenner
REAPER by Larissa Ione
THE SURRENDER GATE by Christopher Rice
SERVICING THE TARGET by Cherise Sinclair
THE LAKE OF LEARNING by Steve Berry and MJ Rose
THE MUSEUM OF MYSTERIES by Steve Berry and MJ Rose

On Behalf of 1001 Dark Nights,

Liz Berry, M.J. Rose, and Jillian Stein would like to thank ~

Steve Berry
Doug Scofield
Benjamin Stein
Kim Guidroz
Social Butterfly PR
Ashley Wells
Asha Hossain
Chris Graham
Chelle Olson
Kasi Alexander
Jessica Johns
Dylan Stockton
Richard Blake
and Simon Lipskar

Made in the USA
Columbia, SC
04 November 2020

23978629R00064